Faith

Hive Honey Quest, Volume 2

Amarah Parks

Published by Amarah Parks LLC, 2024.

FAITH

First edition. August 5, 2024.

Copyright © 2024 Amarah Parks.

ISBN: 979-8224002863

Written by Amarah Parks.

Table of Contents

I dedicate this book to my husband, who helps make it possible for me as a young mom to still pursue creative projects and passions. His support and involvement with family life blesses me greatly. I also dedicate it to God, who pours through me while I create.

FAITH By: Amarah Parks

Chapter 1: Joy and Courage

The wind was crisp but sunkissed. Leaves rustled and sighed in the breeze, promising a change soon. In a few days time, the farm would be filled with bright colors and the smell of earthy air. Flowerwilt was approaching for Hive Honey Quest, and the hive was still hurting from the losses of war.

Royal was soaking in a moment of peace and quiet in her throne room. She drew in a long breath. The last few weeks had been exhausting as she oversaw the healing of her beloved hive. Most able-bodied workers had been recruited to help with the injured after the war ended. Some of the wounded had passed on while others had almost fully recovered. Though the memory of the war was less raw, Royal sensed a deep sadness in the hive. They were disjointed and confused as they tried to find their footing. Hive Honey Quest had changed, and there was a deep vein of uncertainty on what they now stood for. But at least everyone felt safe, and there was an underlying sense of peace and victory that lay beneath it all. *This... this is something we can build from.* Royal felt a bit overwhelmed at the thought, but she knew it was possible. A bright future was within her grasp. *By the grace of Lighthive!*

Royal's contemplative moment was short-lived, as was the norm. Nectar rushed into her room, her furry coat a bit disheveled. She had also been hard at work to help rebuild the hive. "Royal, I hope I'm not interrupting! May I speak with you about some things?"

Royal smiled. "Yes, Nectar. Of course you can." She gathered herself and stood, waiting for Nectar to continue.

"I hope you don't mind if I start with what has been on my heart the most." The queen nodded her permission, and Nectar started, bubbling with passion. "Your Majesty, the dust is settling, and the hive is disconnected. You and I know that Lighthive is our source of peace and unity, but most of the hive has no awareness of it." She paused as Royal listened intently. "How can we help them to feel the vibrations we feel? How can we offer them fulfillment when it only comes from faith, which cannot be forced or rushed?"

Royal paused before responding. "I have been considering this for a while, Nectar. You are correct that faith can't be forced or rushed. We must respect each bee's free will and individual sovereignty. But for those who are seeking, it would be good to provide resources. I have been thinking about ways to help. Do you have any ideas?"

Nectar straightened. "I think it would be helpful to write a book. Something filled with stories and morals. It would be about everything we know regarding Lighthive."

Royal considered this, her face guarded. "I think writings would be incredibly valuable. Testimonies and revelations are powerful. However..." Something felt like it was missing. "I think we would be wise to prioritize relationships first. Can we appoint those who are more connected to Lighthive as mentors?"

Nectar pondered this. "That's a good idea, Royal. I will meditate on that and see if Lighthive has guidance on the subject. Either way, I think it would be wise to work on this very soon. The hive craves leadership and direction. We are vulnerable in this state, as I'm sure you know."

"I do."

She smiled. "I also wanted to let you know that Courage and Joy have just emerged over in the nursery comb. I'm sure you'd like to visit."

"Oh, that's great news!" Royal looked at her nurse bee with gratitude. "Nectar, thank you for all that you do. I couldn't have asked for a better nurse bee."

"Nor I a better queen." Nectar blushed.

Royal beamed, though her thoughts were heavy. She signaled for Nectar to go and share the new information. After taking a moment to compose herself, she decided to make her way to the nursery to meet her new children, her pride and joy as queen of the hive. She had always been more involved with her young than many queens were.

Making the short walk from the throne room, her heart fluttered. She reminisced on the recent difficult laying, in which Joy was trapped behind Courage. She had never experienced anything like that. Eggs were soft and pliable, and there was usually no pain to deliver them. But this egg was sideways. While it should've had no problem turning, it stuck to her like glue. Just when she thought she might die from exhaustion and pain, the egg flipped quickly and effortlessly on its own. It was so strange, and Royal was filled with curiosity about what happened. She wondered if Courage would be different or special somehow. Either way, she couldn't wait to meet her children.

Turning the corner, the nursery comb came into view. In front of it, two young bees stood - one drone and one worker. They looked healthy and eager to take on their tasks in the hive. At the sight of their queen, they dipped their heads, and the caretaker bees who had been talking with the newborns moved aside with respect for their queen.

"Queen Royal!" Joy buzzed excitedly. She was brimming with an undeniable vigor for life, her eyes sparkling with enthusiasm. It seemed like nothing could possibly dim her fire.

"Your Majesty." Courage smiled. His countenance was strong and level. It seemed as if he would not be easily shaken. A quiet confidence emanated from him, somehow harmoniously coinciding with humility and grace.

Taking them in for a hug, Royal beamed. "My children. Joy and Courage. I am honored to finally meet you." She held on for a while before stepping back. "There is much to learn, yes?"

Joy smiled at her mother, her eyes alight. "Yes! It is so exciting to know I have an important role in this place!"

Courage glanced warmly at his sister. "The future is bright!" Lowering his voice, he mumbled to Royal. "Mother... was it me or Joy who was breech?" He shifted a bit, his expression grave.

Royal blinked in confusion. "It was you."

He sighed in shame. "Did I almost kill Joy? And even you?"

"Courage, you were just a tiny egg." The queen beheld her son's face. The hurt he felt was indicative of an old, compassionate soul. She looked at him with wonder. "Son, you can hold no guilt or responsibility for the matter. It simply cannot exist."

"But the pain I caused you... that was real." He clenched his jaw.

Royal touched his face. "I would go through it all again for you." She paused. "Besides, I am still here, aren't I? And your sister is certainly no worse off for it. Don't feel responsible for what you couldn't have caused or controlled."

Courage hesitated, pondering her words. Then he looked at her again with warmth. "Thanks mother. I am glad things are okay now."

Stepping back reluctantly, Royal consulted the caregivers. "We will assign mentors for the new bees soon." She smiled. "But first, one of you girls should take Joy and Courage to the beedances. They should be going on right about now. How about Rain? You may oversee them until their mentors are chosen." She nodded at her new children, her face shining with pride and love. She waved as the caretaker led the newborns away. Royal wished she could stay with them longer, but she was always needed. She stood still for just a moment.

Her mind spun regarding Courage's concern. *He felt guilty for being sideways!* While an honorable and considerate thought, it was a bit silly as well. He had just been an egg, helpless to control his state of being. Still, her heart was touched by his maturity to think outside of himself at such a young age. *Not many think this way so early on. And Joy as well... both are so unwavering and refreshing.* She knew that each would become valuable members of the hive, and she couldn't wait to get to know them more.

With that, Royal headed back to the throne room. There never was a dull moment as Queen of the hive, after all.

Chapter 2: The Beedances

*W*iggle, Waggle, Shake Shake Shake, Figure Eight, Waggle, Wag! Joy watched closely, trying to memorize the sequence. *Wiggle, Waggle, Shake Shake Shake, Figure Eight, Waggle, Wag!* The dance was already spreading like wildfire. Her caregiver Rain gestured encouragingly for her to try. Taking a deep breath, she went for it. She wiggled, waggled, and shook. *Figure Eight, Waggle Wag!* It was absolutely on point. Rain watched in amazement as each step fell perfectly. Some other workers began forming around Joy as she repeated the steps. As soon as she finished, they too mirrored the sequence. In no time, the dance had successfully been communicated throughout the entire landing grounds.

"Wow Joy, excellent job! Most bees don't catch on so quickly during their very first beedance." Rain praised her. Much of the crowd of bees began filing out of the hive's entrance on a quest for honey. The beedances weren't just for enjoyment purposes. Every move communicated directions to an ideal source of nectar. It was essential that the message was spread accurately and effectively, especially so late in the season when nectar started to become more scarce.

A small, dispersing crowd cheered for Joy as well, and a few workers nearby exclaimed:

"I've never seen a beginner dance so well!"

"Way to go!"

Courage parted his way through the crowd toward his sister. "Joy, you are a natural!" He smiled.

"Thanks Courage! I don't know, I just did it. I didn't think too hard." She blushed.

"I think that's the definition of natural." Rain laughed. "You did amazingly."

The siblings' caregiver began mingling with some of the bees left in the clearing. The setting was casual and relaxed, and Joy and Courage enjoyed the breather. They moved over to the edge of the clearing and just sat together. Joy smiled at her brother in admiration.

"I am glad to have a brother like you." Joy was the type to say exactly what she felt without holding back.

Courage looked at her with love. "I feel like the luckier sibling. It's nice having each other while we navigate this new life. What a blessing."

Joy was pleased with his response, and rested her head on her brother's shoulder. "Do you think we will do big things in this hive? I hope so! I want to make a difference. I want to make everyone feel loved and blessed like I am."

He laughed softly. "I think we will. Especially if we focus on doing what's right." After a moment, Courage stood up. "I'm going to check with Rain and make sure there's nothing we should be doing. I'll be right back!" He paced over to the small group of workers near the center of the landing grounds.

Joy sat motionless, just taking in the usual hustle and bustle of the hive. She loved the way the hive ran. It was so intricately operated, and yet run by instinct. Everyone seemed to know exactly what they needed to do. She was lost in thought when suddenly she heard someone talking to her on her right side.

"Hey, those were some nice moves!" Joy turned to face an older worker bee. She seemed friendly and self-assured. "I'm Goldenrod, but you can call me Goldie. What's your name?"

"Oh, I'm Joy! Sorry, I didn't notice you there!" Joy shifted, embarrassed that she hadn't been aware of the worker's presence.

"You're new here, right?" Goldie asked.

"Yeah, I just hatched today." Joy laughed. "It's nice to meet you. What is your job in the hive?"

Goldie smiled. "I do a lot of things, including some of the very same things you will do, like harvesting nectar, making honey, and enjoying the comradery of the hive." Goldie sat by Joy. "I also help with a nice group of bees here. Kind of like a club."

Joy perked up. "Oh? What for?"

"We like to focus on the betterment of ourselves and the hive. Sometimes we come up with good ideas that leadership could use. But mostly, we enjoy the community and friendship we share together. Does that sound like something you'd enjoy?" Goldie looked at her unblinkingly.

"It sounds nice!" Joy buzzed. "What's it called?"

"We like to refer to the group as 'New Beginning', but there's no official name really. We just focus on each other." Goldie handed Joy a small piece of birch bark. "If you ever want to come, here's the info. You would fit right in!"

Joy looked down at the card, which had times, dates, names, and contact information. "Oh, thanks! I'll think about it! I am pretty focused on my training right now, but maybe in a few days I can swing by."

"Whenever you can. We can teach you a lot as well, if you are interested. We could use your moves at our smaller beedances." Goldie paused. "Anyway, it was great meeting you. I hope to talk again!" The worker turned and flew off.

Joy rested into her thoughts. *I could never have expected to be so well received on my first day. Everyone is so nice! Especially Goldie! I wonder when I could get to one of these meetings.* She smiled to herself. *I get to figure out who I am and what my purpose is on this earth. And maybe I'll make some new friends too.* Joy was such an optimist, and she knew that everyone around her was as genuine as she. She felt safe here. She felt at home.

"Joy, sorry I took so long!" Courage spoke suddenly. "I got caught up in conversation. Rain actually needs us now; the crowd has dispersed."

NECTAR EYED HER AUDIENCE carefully. *Who would Lighthive appoint to mentor the hive?* Before her was a small group of bees who had been more seasoned in life experience and awareness of Lighthive. Among them were Love, Trust, Peace, Faith, Hope, General Pollen, and Sweet Pea. Nectar had already explained to them the purpose of this gathering, and was now quietly awaiting guidance. The workers peered up at her, filled with anticipation.

Sweet Pea is not ready. Her faith is so new, while full of vigor. She has much growth to be had before taking a position of spiritual leadership. Pollen has only recently acknowledged Lighthive by its name, but she is old and wise. It is clear she has felt its vibrations for much longer than we know. The sisters each have valuable insight and wisdom to share. Of course Hope will... What? Lighthive, are you sure? Nectar scratched her chin curiously. Sometimes Lighthive still surprised her, even after all this time. *And me... really? What an honor...* Sorting out her thoughts, she opened her mouth to speak.

"Ladies, Lighthive has chosen some of you to be mentors for the hive, and others to contribute in other ways, such as writings or management. First off, I will reveal the chosen mentors." She paused. "Lighthive has appointed me, Love, Pollen, and..." *What? You waited until this moment to tell me?* "And Courage?" Her voice trailed off almost like a question. *But he was only hatched yesterday!* She looked up at the ceiling in confusion. And yet, she was used to surprises from Lighthive.

"Me?" Pollen was completely shocked. She lowered her gaze to the ground with humility. "I am... honored, though this is quite a responsibility. I hope Lightive is right."

"Of course Lighthive is right. Has it ever been wrong before?" Love patted Pollen's shoulder reassuringly. Her expression was tender and kind.

The others stayed silent, bewildered. Courage? He was a newborn with no knowledge!

Nectar seemed to sort herself out. "You are all probably as surprised as I am," she grunted, straightening. "As for those who will contribute in other smaller ways, Lighthive has appointed the following. Peace, Faith, and Trust."

The group stayed silent, expecting Nectar to continue. Moments passed. When she did not add another name, they looked at each other in disbelief.

"And Hope?" Peace offered.

"Not Hope." Nectar responded, her voice laced with genuine compassion. "I don't understand how or why Lighthive appoints us, but that is what I gathered."

Hope appeared shocked. Not just shocked, but visibly hurt, and a little angry. She seemed to have certainly not expected this outcome. Pea was next to her. She appeared even a bit relieved that she was not chosen. Perhaps she didn't feel ready. She rested a hand on Hope, whispering *I'm sorry.* Hope looked vexed now, and she silently shrugged Pea's hand away.

"Lighthive has spoken!" Nectar concluded. "As for Courage, I feel it is not time yet to tell him or anyone else. We will allow him to complete his week of training first. Those of you who were appointed as mentors - come with me on a trip to the Honeycrystal immediately to connect with Lighthive. For now, the rest of you can go. We will talk soon."

The room buzzed quietly with chatter as the chosen bees shared their excitement and fears. Hope left the room promptly, Pea just behind her.

Chapter 3: A Second Prophecy

Courage trembled with excitement and anticipation. Royal had just selected Joy's trainer, and she had gone to begin learning. Now, it was his turn. Deep down, he had a powerful and unquenching desire to make a difference in his lifetime. *As soon as I have some instruction to build upon, I will be one step closer to making that difference.*

"And Courage, you will be instructed by Thistle. Iris will also aid in your training. They both served honorably in the War of the Ghost, and have a close bond of friendship. They work well together, and I trust them with your instruction." Royal smiled at her son, her eyes sparkling with pride and a trace of wonder.

Courage dipped his head and watched as two strapping drones parted their way through the crowd to meet him. The slightly shorter drone extended his arm. "Courage, it is our honor to train you. I am Thistle, and this is Iris."

"It's great to meet you both!"

Royal stepped down from her stage, King Sting at her side. "Congratulations, drones." The King also offered his congratulations.

"Thank you, Your Majesties. Where should we begin?" Thistle asked.

"I would like you to start by helping Courage understand and envision the War of the Ghost, our recent history. Take him to the battle grounds. There, you can also train him in some combat. Start without weapons at first. Before his training is complete, he should know the farm and its boundaries, and should meet members of the wild hive - our treasured allies. Report his progress to Orchid, and she will get it to me." Royal paused. "Toward the end of his training this week, you should find a way to test him on his knowledge, skill level, and moral compass. I trust you will ensure all three are present and plentiful."

Thistle and Iris nodded before gesturing to Courage to follow them. They took off toward the hive's entrance, which emanated with such brightness, he needed to squint. *I wonder what it looks like outside?* As they passed by the hive guards, it took several seconds for his eyes to adjust. When they did, he immediately felt at home. Nature was beautiful.

His instincts were keenly aware of his surroundings, even though he had never been told the names of things. *Trees, flowers, a branch, leaves, oh, and that! Wind.* Courage enjoyed the flight, delightedly stretching his wings. He squinted up at the source of light. *Sun... "The light in the sky that allows us to see..."* He remembered one of the caregivers telling him about it after he had hatched. *"...to see creation in its beauty. In the evening, it casts away its fiery rays. It scatters its specks of light across the whole sky, leaving the sun itself bare and dim. Then it is called 'moon'. In the early morning, it begins to gather its rays little by little until it covers the world once again in light."* Courage couldn't picture it before. He was awestruck in its mighty presence. *"The sun is another daily reminder to let the Light guide us."*

As Courage was peering toward the sky, Thistle and Iris stopped, alighting on a branch. Courage joined them, eager to begin his training. "We'd like to start by adding to your knowledge of the war." Thistle began.

HOPE SMILED WEAKLY at her friend. Sweet Pea could always make everybee feel a little better.

"Nectar didn't choose bees based on her own opinions. She seemed just as surprised as we were. I don't think she did anything maliciously." Pea was an optimist. "I'm glad I wasn't chosen personally. That's a lot of pressure, and I'm definitely not that confident yet! But I was honored to be considered."

Hope brooded. "I don't know, whoever decided has some strange thought processes. I can't believe a newborn was chosen for a high, influential position, and I'm not even allowed to contribute." She scoffed. "It just doesn't seem like Lighthive made the right choice." *I honestly doubt Lighthive's competence in general right now.*

Pea's eyes grew wide. "I think there's a lot we don't understand, and may never understand. But Lighthive sees so much that we don't see. We just have to trust, I think."

Hope nodded blankly. She wasn't convinced. *It just doesn't feel quite right with Lighthive. I don't feel connected to it, or appreciated by it. There has to be a way to understand. I don't like being in the dark about things. I like to know.* "Well Pea, I appreciate you. I think I need to go off and process for a bit. Maybe I'll go pollinate or something."

"Ok Hope. I'm here for you if you need me!" Pea smiled at her friend.

"Thanks." Hope buzzed away, her mind spinning. She had always been a more emotional and introspective bee, and deep down, she was searching for something constant. Something she could understand and rely on. She knew Lighthive was real, but she wasn't sure how real it felt to her. *I want something that's real for me.* She was so busy thinking that she didn't notice a bee had sat next to her.

"You look like you've got a lot on your mind." It was a worker bee. Her expression was compassionate.

"Oh!" Hope jumped a little. "Hi. I mean, yes. Just doubting some things."

"I can tell that you are a deep thinker. That's a good thing. What's your name?"

NECTAR KEPT SEEING flashbacks of the way Hope's eyes had rounded, her mouth agape. There was a burning in her eyes. Confusion, resentment even. Nectar had never seen Hope in this way before. She had always been kind, friendly, and hard-working, and she was even a respected war hero. *She was born with a lot on her plate, and had an understandable reaction to that. Otherwise, she has been a good friend and hivemate. She has been dedicated and even wise.* Nectar didn't understand. If she had been choosing mentors for the hive, Hope would have certainly been one of them.

She isn't ready. Nectar heard once again. *Okay, I get the message!* She chuckled coarsely to herself, then sighed gravely as Hope's face kept flashing in her mind. The war was over, but now the hive was facing a war within. This kind of war could be even more deadly. *Oh Lighthive, I pray this inner turmoil won't overcome us!* She sat silently for several moments, when suddenly she perked up as Lightive spoke.

"Beware, a gem of brilliant light,
Will cast a ray so very bright,
All in it's path may no longer see,
Blinding every passing bee.
But there are few who will see through
Those deadly, holy rays,
Through faith as strong as iron, they
Will fight the evil ways."

Chapter 4: Before the Frost

*C*ourage drifted through a powerful air current confidently. *I'm really getting the hang of these wings!* He was a few days into his training, and today his instructors were taking him to the northern boundary. The wild hive had asked for help. Their job was to go and gather the details in order to relay the information to Queen Royal. Then, she could decide who and how many to send for their aid.

Thistle and Iris were unrelenting in their pace. The two were really putting Courage's speed to the test. Sometimes they would even make unnecessary detours to observe his reflexes and maneuvering abilities. "That's it!" Thistle shouted affirmingly as Courage displayed his prowess. The farm flashed beside them in a blur. Before long, the three drones had reached the edge of Ally Forest, the wild hive's wood.

Iris gasped for breath. "You two keep me young!" The three bumped each other playfully, letting out some whoops and chuckles.

Thistle collected himself to begin teaching. "So, we are at the edge of Honey Quest territory now. The Hive of Soldiers runs regular boundary patrols, so we respect their space by not barging in. Always stop at the edge of the wood and wait to be intercepted." He paused. "However, there is one occasion where you don't need to wait. When you visit the Honeycrystal, there is a certain path you can take without being disrespectful. It's a highway of sorts. On normal occasions, no one will attempt to stop or intercept you there."

Courage nodded. "Do we run border patrols for Hive Honey Quest?"

Thistle shook his head. "We have more than enough food sources, so we don't have to gatekeep them. Wild hives have historically been pushed out by domestic hives like ours, so they often have to be more purposeful about their territory if they want to make it. This wild hive is pretty established. Every member does their part." The three waited silently for a few moments. Almost as if on cue, a scruffy looking drone confronted them.

"And who might you be?" He held himself tall and strong, with an air of authority. Courage was immediately glad he wasn't an enemy.

"We've come from Hive Honey Quest, responding to your request for aid." Iris offered. Members of the wild hive spoke very eloquently, and responded well to the same. Courage noted how his mentor slightly adjusted his way of speaking to relate to this wild hive member.

The strange drone cocked his head. His suspicion had waned, but wasn't completely gone. "What is the name of your Queen, and ours?"

"Queen Royal, and Queen Shanelle." Thistle was quick and confident in his response. The drone seemed satisfied with that, and gestured for the three to follow him. He wordlessly led them into the woods.

Courage was excited to see the wild hive. He had heard brief descriptions, but something told him it would be more incredible in person. *It's amazing that they are so well established without any help or intervention. They are strong.* While being a domestic hive had its downsides, there were many ways in which Honeybandits helped preserve the hive as well. But it seemed to Courage that the wild hive had been established and independant for quite some time. He wondered what they could possibly need their help with. After weaving through trees for a while, they finally approached the hive. It was every bit as amazing as Courage had expected.

They neared a strong, living oak with a cavity in which the wild hive was built. Courage could hardly take it all in as the four drones rushed through its grand entrance. The wild hive was shockingly intricate and winding in its construction. There were no straight lines, but instead, spirals of comb molded to the shape of the hollowed tree. Courage wished he could linger, but the wild drone was leading them to the throne room at the top of the hive with impressive speed and dexterity. *This is the most inaccessible, protected area. Brilliant.* Courage felt a strange familiarity with the feeling in this hive that he couldn't place. One way or another, it truly fascinated him.

Their guide stopped abruptly at the entrance to the throne room. "This is where I bid you adieu. I am not a part of these proceedings, and must resume patrol duties. Sir Taves will meet you here." With that, he departed.

Courage, Thistle, and Iris waited patiently together for a few moments. *I get to meet Sir Taves, a prominent war hero!* After about five minutes, an aging warrior greeted them from inside the doorway. Despite his old legs, he moved like a newborn, without lagging. This was the first time Courage had seen a drone with clear signs of age.

"Greetings! Thank you for coming swiftly." Sir Taves flashed a dazzling smile, which was his trademark. 'Everyone who flew beside him in battle had noted his feel-good countenance', Courage remembered Thistle saying.

"Greetings!" Thistle dipped his head respectfully. "We are here to learn how we can help you."

Sir Taves' sunny smile faded. "Yes. There is much at hand right now." He paced a moment before leading the group to a table with acorn shell chairs. "Sit." The group stayed quiet, acknowledging the drone's grave expression. He took a breath, and began.

"Men, I'm going to be straightforward. The cold season approaches rapidly. For us, and most honey bee hives, there is another event that takes place at this time of year... This is the purging of drones."

Courage felt a chill down his spine. He knew his home was unusual in that the drones lived longer lives. But in most hives, drones lived only a couple of months. If they still lived this late in the year, they would be forcibly cast out from the hive. They had no further purpose, and if kept within, would just be unnecessary mouths to feed. He knew all of this, and yet it didn't make this topic any less chilling for him.

"This will occur by the first frost. We are pinning down a date for the event now."

"Even for you?" Courage interjected. "I'm sorry for interrupting you. This is all new to me."

Sir Taves smiled. "Yes, even for me. See, in most hives, this is simply the nature of things. I am honored to leave so that the Queen and her daughters have the best chance at survival. It is something most of us embrace honorably." His expression grew dark again. "Others, not so much. There's a larger than usual band of drones this year who will try to go unnoticed. If they were to succeed, their numbers could seriously threaten the hive. However, we are already one step ahead of them. This is where we hope Hive Honey Quest comes in."

The guest drones exchanged glances uneasily before Sir Taves continued.

"We need to draw these drones away from the hive right as we are going to close our doors." Sir Taves paused awkwardly. "We know it's a lot to ask, but we want Queen Royal to visit our drone congregation area."

Courage, Thistle, and Theo gasped. *The drone congregation area? This was a place where drones hung out hoping to meet queens who had no mate. Queen Royal has a mate! And we don't know what these drones are like. It could be dangerous for her. In fact, simply leaving the hive is extremely dangerous for her!* He was shocked.

"You know that this is quite a lot to ask of us," Thistle spoke gravely. "We would be risking our Queen - our very livelihood - to save you some roughhousing."

Sir Taves' eyes flashed. "It is a lot to ask, I won't deny, but we will *not* remove hive members forcibly. Most of us believe in our duty as drones to remove ourselves. But these drones would stay and risk the well-being of our entire family. Due to the particularly large group this time, we simply must keep them from freeloading off of the women's hard work of gathering food all year. They need to go. I can assure you that the bees we need removed will jump at the opportunity to meet a queen, and will go knowing full well that their lives could be lost."

Thistle contemplated gravely. "I cannot promise that Queen Royal will agree to this task, but I will relay the message to her. I'll be sure that someone updates you on our answer." He took a breath. "We are an alliance, and Hive Honey Quest wants to help you. We just need to decide if we are willing to risk it all to do so."

Sir Taves nodded. "We have brainstormed options tirelessly and this would be the best way. We regret having to ask this of you... If all of our drones understood their duty and honor, this wouldn't even be an issue. But we do ask one thing for certain. If Royal can't help in this way, then we would hope for her help in coming up with the right solution, and fast." Sir Taves' expression was eager and passionate.

"How many drones are we talking about here?" Iris chimed in.

"There are a couple hundred or so."

Iris' jaw dropped. "How would we protect our queen? We don't know how they would treat her."

Sir Taves smiled. "You would need to send a sizable group of your own. There should be at least a hundred workers around the queen to protect her, and possibly undercover drones in the crowd as well, to intervene if needed. We need to do this soon. The plan would be a week from now." He paused. "I know you will try to help, because we have done the same for you - risking it all." Though his words were assuming, his tone of voice was optimistic and innocent. There was no trace of manipulation or domination. If anything, it was laced with hope.

Thistle bowed his head. "Sir Taves, we will relay this request to our Queen and make you aware of her decision forthrightly." Then the Soldier escorted the three to the front of the hive to begin the flight home.

"Thank you for your consideration!" Sir Taves flashed a wide grin and waved.

"Farewell!" Courage called out as they left. After flying away for a few quiet minutes, he buzzed to Thistle and Iris. "Wow. Our lives are so different from theirs. It almost feels wrong, and yet *we* are the ones who defy nature."

Thistle was contemplative. "I get what you are saying. Think of their hive though. Drones usually have a short-lived purpose in this life, and if they stay, may doom more important members to starve. Maybe even the queen. Most hives will mercilessly throw drones out to their deaths when it gets cold, or even kill them."

"I just don't know how deception is better than that. They'd be better off just exiling the extra drones in my opinion." Iris chimed in.

"The drones who go to a congregation area are making a conscious choice to leave, and are already prepared to die. Must I remind you that naturally, drones don't meet their children?" Thistle interjected. "Typically those who find a mate die immediately."

Courage sighed. "Perhaps we are really the twisted ones. How is it that we aren't subject to the design of nature?"

Thistle looked at Courage curiously. "You know, you are a deep thinker. I'm not sure how we came to be this way, but I see our plight as a blessing and a curse. Because we continue to live when other drones don't, we ought to do more to contribute to the well-being of the hive. We may live longer and have the pleasure of friendship - even love, but our lives are dedicated to training and the protection of our hive. The wild hive trains many drones to be warriors, but in most hives, drones just eat. They don't protect, care for the young, or forage. Life is simple and easy, and their purpose is clear."

"Our lives aren't as simple, it seems. We have to find our purpose, and do whatever we can to contribute so we don't just take, take, take." Iris added.

Find our purpose... Courage pondered these words. "I still don't know what's right or wrong to me in this situation, but I hope part of my purpose can be to help in some way. Hopefully Lighthive will guide us on what to do."

ROYAL STOOD BEFORE thousands of bees gathered in the landing grounds. She had called a meeting to speak about the mentors Lighthive had appointed. "I ask that all of you might speak with one of the appointed mentors to help with your questions." She paused. So many eyes were on her, burning into her skin. Some were clueless, and others were cold as stone. Still, many were seeking and hopeful. *At least some of them might come to know Lighthive and feel its vibrations within.* "The mentors are Pollen, Nectar, and Love. One more will be appointed by the end of the week. You can also ask Trust, Peace, or Faith to connect you with the mentors and schedule your meeting with one of them. The mentors will be stationed in the cells near my throne room from sunrise to sunset, five days a week, starting tomorrow. They will rest on Wednesdays and Sundays. Please attempt to meet with them at least once before the frost comes."

A worker bee parted through the crowd toward the front. "Queen Royal, is meeting with a mentor mandatory for all?" Her voice was challenging.

"No one will be forced to do so, but I plead with you all to give it one shot. If you like it, you can continue meeting with the mentors long-term." Royal responded, looking down at the worker. She was passionate, no doubt. Passionate and rigid. *Some bees here may see the Light and walk in the other direction.* Her heart hurt to think of that. She wanted every bee to know the Light she rested in. Royal concluded quietly and stepped down from her pedestal.

Chapter 5: The Trip to the Honeycrystal

Pollen, Nectar, and Love had begun their journey to the Honeycrystal in order to prepare and equip themselves for the task at hand - mentorship. *It's no small thing, for certain...* Pollen thought. She would possibly be one of few to truly see and acknowledge bees who were seeking. She would have to give advice and offer hope to them, and that sort of thing was a big responsibility. The last thing Pollen wanted to do was mislead someone or fall short. The group had remained introspective for much of the journey, just taking in the sounds of nature and preparing their minds to meet with Lighthive.

"What's it like at the Honeycrystal?" Pollen asked, breaking the silence.

Love responded. "I've been there. There are many tunnels to navigate on the way in, and a great hollowed room where it sits. When the sun illuminates the crystal, it's the brightest light you can imagine. I haven't rested on it yet, or received a dream. All I know is that Hope was literally glowing afterwards, and muttering words of wisdom. Sir Taves said that the first time can be more disorienting."

Nectar added. "After we rest on the crystal, we should stay silent in the chamber. We can speak again once we have exited the tunnels."

"Are we meant to share what we learn or keep it inside?" Pollen buzzed.

Nectar smiled. "Some things will remain personal, to be held within. Others are to be proclaimed from the treetops. You will know what things are to be shared or not shared. After today, your connection to Lighthive will be stronger and will feel more real - even more real than your existence now."

Pollen took in those words. *I still don't know what Lighthive sees in me. But I am beyond excited to find out how I can help.* Pollen was older now. She had spent much of her life under tyrannical leadership, and now she was free to pursue her faith. Still, there had always been a vibration within that she could not deny. She lived by it. She was anxious to meet with Lighthive. *Whatever that may mean...* Her brain could hardly wrap around it as it was. *I'm ready for it to feel even more real.*

The three workers reached the edge of the forest. Ahead, the mountain was in sight. "Not far now!" Love was enthusiastic. "I am so happy to be back, and to finally have my own experience."

Pollen gasped at the spectacular view. The mountain was grand, and the gorge below cradled a beautiful waterfall that danced along the edge of a lush forest. The other riverbank held a glorious meadow full of every kind of flower. It was heavenly, like its own world. They could see it all, and yet it still appeared far away, as if they would never reach it. Nectar began leading the group upward, and Pollen reluctantly peeled away from the breathtaking view to follow suit.

As they ascended, the wind was almost unbearable. *Wow, it sure is no small feat to get to this stone!* It seemed like an hour had passed as they exerted every muscle in their bodies to the limit. Just when Pollen thought she might plummet to the earth from the cold and exhaustion, the cliff's edge gave way, exposing a small cave. The group landed on a flat walkway with relief. "Wow! What a journey!" Pollen exclaimed enthusiastically after catching her breath for a moment.

"It certainly is!" Nectar panted, nodding to Pollen and Love. She looked back at the cave's entrance with urgency. "Lighthive bless!" She cried. "The sun has found its peak! We need to hurry." Without hesitation she led the girls through a network of tunnels. The correct path was so brightly lit that Pollen almost didn't notice the various wrong turns lurking in the shadows. *I wonder where they lead...* Pollen pressed on until the three reached their destination.

"We made it!" Love cried, clearly brimming with excitement. The stone was brightly lit and blinding. Wordlessly, the girls went to the stone's edge, climbed upon it, and found a spot to lie down. Pollen was the last to settle atop the amber stone. Almost immediately as she closed her eyes, she was swept away.

Pollen panicked as she felt herself submerged in cold, rushing waters. The churning current dangerously held her down as she struggled for her life. Her head emerged for just long enough to cry out. "Help!" She was swept under again. Suddenly, as Pollen's limbs froze up with shock and fear, something large and strong retrieved her from the water in a single swipe. She gasped for air as she was rescued from the depths, only to peer at her rescuer in terror. *A bird?!* The large, feathered creature held her in his beak. His grasp was firm, but careful. He carried her to the riverbank before releasing the helpless bug from his grasp. He placed her delicately on a patch of lush moss.

"Hello?" The bird squawked carefreely.

Pollen dried her face and looked up at the creature with disdain. He was fairly large, strong in body, and was clad in mostly dark feathers. "I suppose you're going to eat me now?" She trembled. The bird tilted his head at her curiously, not answering. In his hesitation, she glanced around her in wonder. *Where... am I?* Much to her surprise, the scene looked a lot like the view she had seen as they began scaling the mountain. Except now, she was in it. She allowed her jaw to drop as she took it all in. "How did I get here? And who are you?"

The creature jerked toward her in a very bird-like fashion, closely inspecting her face. "Well, let me see. How you got here, I am not so very sure. But I do know that I am Bravewing, a messenger of Lighthive. And you are Pollen." He flashed an awkward smile as he twitched about. "And do not fear, you are no one's lunch here. But, maybe we can fly together."

"Oh, I'm completely soak..." Pollen glanced down at herself in awe, suddenly realizing she was totally dry and warm. "How?" She shook her head in amazement. "Wait, you know me?"

"It's my first time being a messenger, and your first time being, well, here."

"What kind of bird are you?" Pollen asked, shaking her nerves.

"I am a sparrow. Perhaps you and I can explore the scenery. You arrived a bit later than expected, so we must make the most of the time we have. Here, climb on. It'll be quicker." Bravewing gestured for Pollen to fly up onto his back. She obliged, though a bit uneasily. Without hesitation he took off. Pollen grasped onto the down of his feathers for dear life as he ascended.

As they rose above the enchantingly beautiful gorge, Pollen eagerly took it all in. "This place is other-worldly. I can't even believe my eyes!"

"It certainly is beautiful!" Bravewing chirped pleasantly. The gorge emanated a powerful peace, reminiscent of the peace within that Pollen had felt in smaller measures before. But here, it was perfect and complete. All was well.

"Do bees always have to come through the river when they visit?" Pollen shuddered.

Bravewing glanced up at her, his head sideways. "Well, let's see. You have visited the sunrock, but all newcomers arrive here differently. And it is my job to look after you while you are here. This place is full of surprises. You may not always come the same way, or, you might."

Just then, a vibrant green hummingbird passed by them. It hesitated, hovering in flight for just a moment. "Greetings Bravewing!"

"Greetings Humblewing!" The sparrow nodded curtly to imply his rushed manner, and the hummingbird continued past them cheerily.

This place is teeming with creatures that might enjoy a bee for a snack, including Bravewing. And yet, they coexist in perfect harmony. What a place. Pollen held on, eager to see where her guide would take her and to learn what he'd tell her. After a few more minutes, the sparrow landed on a branch that bent under his weight. He stared ahead with reverence. Pollen peered in the same direction. They had landed at the top of a tree that stood taller than any of the others, and they could see the gray mountainside and crashing waterfall. The sun hit it all in the perfect kind of light. The whole valley glowed like it was golden hour.

Then, Pollen noticed the light illuminating what appeared to be a crack in the mountainside. It extended from the base of the mountain all the way to its peak. The more she focused on it, the brighter and more obvious it glared. "What is that?"

"Do you see it?" Bravewing squawked excitedly. "Not everyone can. The heart of Lighthive shines so brightly that it leaves absolutely no room for darkness. You must know this Light to be able to see its heart." He shook his wings, pleased. "I am lucky to be your messenger, because you know the Light."

Pollen had to squint as the rays illuminated the whole scene. "Wow! I've never seen so much and so little at the same time!" She chuckled good-naturedly. "Who can't see that? It seems like it'd be hard to miss!"

Bravewing smiled quickly. "More than you'd realize! Most will see it part of the time, and choose to look away before it grows. But when one stays focused on it, it illuminates every part of them. It exposes every shadow and cleanses all it touches. If you allow it to work, it leaves no stone unturned."

Pollen had been taking in the Light. After a while, it began to feel like too much. She felt completely naked and vulnerable under its rays. She blinked and shook her head. "It is hard to keep looking."

"Yes, it is. It is the hardest, most vulnerable, and most freeing path to take. One day, you will be able to dwell within it without a care." The bird tilted his head to look at Pollen again. "You know, you fit in here. Perhaps one day you will choose to be a messenger."

The worker glanced at him. "Me? A messenger of Lighthive?" She shook her head in disbelief. "How could I? My faith is so new."

"No, your faith is not new at all." The sparrow interjected. "You've harbored it for a long time. You've just learned its name."

Pollen felt tears fall down her cheeks. "This is home."

"The Light is with you always. The Light is your home." The two winged creatures sat in silence as the sun crept across the sky.

"Bravewing, how am I going to mentor so many bees who are seeking? How can I help them to find the Light?"

"Bear the Light, and let it transform all you do, think, and say. Don't withhold any part of yourself from it. Then, anyone around you will see. You might see me in your dreams more often now, too! I'll help however I can." At that moment, Bravewing twitched as he stared at the sky. "We must be going now, Pollen. Our time is up." Without warning, he took off toward the mountain.

Pollen closed her eyes and rode the waves in her stomach with the sudden altitude change. As the sparrow flew with great speed, the sound of the waterfall became more and more deafening. Bravewing shook his feathers to rouse her. She opened her eyes with dismay as she saw they were hovering directly over the waterfall. The bird pointed his beak toward the water with urgency. "What? I'm meant to dive in?" Pollen was shocked. The bird did not relent. She took a hurried breath before jumping off his back with abandoned trust and plummeting downwards.

Just as her body hit the water, she found herself stirring on the surface of the Honeycrystal. The sunlight quickly drained from its surface as the workers climbed down, their faces awe-struck.

Chapter 6: New Beginning

Joy was resting in her cell. It had been a long day of training, and she was tired. She glanced down at the card in her hand. *Maybe I can muster some energy to attend tonight's meeting.* The kind bee, Goldie, had really encouraged her to come. Joy was optimistic and excited to make some new friends. She took a breath and decided to go.

The meeting was being held in an out-of-the-way part of the hive that she rarely went to. She had a little trouble finding it, actually. But after about ten minutes of working her way through the halls, she found the meeting. She entered a room of at least a hundred bees. Joy wasn't sure where to go or who to talk to, since Goldie was nowhere in sight. *Wow. I feel out of place.* She laughed quietly at her own social anxiety as she entered the crowd. Every bee who saw her smiled broadly. *They are so welcoming!* Suddenly, the hustle and bustle of the crowd went silent.

On a pedestal in the front, Goldie stood ready to speak. Everyone listened intently. "Welcome bees! Thank you for coming to tonight's meeting! We are a place of new beginnings and friendship. Are you seeking purpose in your life? Do you feel lonely in this big hive? We are a family." The crowd cheered in response. "Tonight, we will be having some practice beedances! We will help you all learn new moves so you can shine on the dance floor. But before we begin, everyone please turn and say hello to your neighbor!"

A worker next to Joy turned to her, smiling widely. "Hey! I'm Rika. What's your name?"

"I'm Joy!"

"Nice to meet you! Hey, I recognize you. Aren't you a great dancer or something? Tonight will be a piece of cake for you!"

Joy blushed. "Well, I suppose!" She studied Rika. The she-bee had a string of flower seeds adorning her waist as a skirt.

She did a little spin to show off the way it flowed. "You like my skirt? We will have to make you one just like it! Only our most skilled members get this kind." Rika posed, displaying the skirt proudly. "You'd look just wonderful in this!"

"Thanks!" Joy was starting to feel a bit uncomfortable with receiving so much praise.

Rika looked around her. "You know, Joy, this group is a lot more than just pretty skirts and great dancing. Like Goldie said, we're a family. A lot of us never felt like we fit in before. But now, we have tons of great friends. I can hardly imagine missing an event anymore! I'd go crazy without it!" Rika let out a coarse chuckle.

There was something off about her expression. Joy began feeling a little uneasy. *Everyone here is so nice... like oddly so. It's almost too much.* She looked around warily as the music began to play. Several young bees like herself were herded to the center of the dancefloor to receive instruction. Joy slipped through the crowd and watched from a distance. Several skirted workers were showing the young bees dance moves Joy had never seen before. She looked around at the bees surrounding the dancefloor, studying them. They didn't look as cheery as they stood in the shadow of the dance lights. *I don't know what it is, but something just feels a little off here.*

Joy peered into the center of the floor again and spotted a familiar bee. She wasn't a youngster, but she was in the crowd of newcomers being instructed. It was Hope! *Oh, interesting!* Joy waited to feel more relaxed, but her spirit remained unsettled. Eventually she decided to slip out and retire early to her cell. Joy was confused by her own thoughts. She couldn't tell if it was just some anxiety, or if her gut was trying to tell her something. Either way, she figured it would help to sleep it off. On her way to her cell, she ran into her dear brother.

"Courage!" Joy flew to her brother and gave him a warm hug. "It's good to see you! How was your training today?"

Courage looked happy to see his sister. "Joy!" He smiled. "Training was good. We visited the wild hive! Now Thistle and Iris are reporting information to the queen."

"Oh wow, it sounds important!" Joy paused. "I mostly just explored the farm and pollinated flowers today! Nectar is such a tasty treat. We've been storing honey in various places throughout the hive to prepare for Flowersleep. My mentors say that the Honeybandits only take from the large frames."

"Who is teaching you?" Courage asked.

"My mentor is actually Sweet Pea! But Queen Royal also assigned a younger bee named Flower to help. She is full of vigor, that one!" Joy laughed. "I'm having lots of fun."

"It's amazing how much we have to learn in just seven days! But by the end of this, we will be ready to serve the hive." Courage swelled with pride. "I can't wait to find out what my role here will be."

Joy looked at her brother in admiration. "No doubt it will be something really honorable!" She paused. "I just got back from an extracurricular social gathering. I was so tired but thought I'd give it a try."

"And?" Courage buzzed.

"Well, it was..." Joy tried to find the words. She looked up into Courage's eyes. "Everything seemed so lovely. But for some reason, something just felt off. Maybe it was me being in my head, but either way, I decided to leave early."

Courage searched her expression. "Interesting. Well, the gut doesn't lie, sister. I'm glad you listened, just in case!" He touched her shoulder. "And hey, I'm your brother. I love you, and I'm here for you if you ever want company."

"Thanks." Joy beamed. "I didn't recognize anyone else at the entire meeting, except for one. Hope. Isn't she one of Royal's oldest daughters?"

Courage looked a bit troubled. "Yes, I believe so. Hopefully there's nothing weird going on. If there is, we might need to rescue her!" He laughed it off.

"Have you been connecting with your mentors?" Joy changed the subject.

Courage lit up. "Yes, I really have! Thistle and Iris have quickly become close friends of mine. Did you know Thistle has a brother? His name is Theo. He's in the hive, but he fought against the resistance in most of the war. He ended up betraying Buzzz at the last minute and switching sides! Still, Thistle says it's a complicated relationship. So if my mentor is ever down, he's probably pining after his brother and the bond he wants to have. Iris, on the other hand, is impossible to distract. He's intense, but it keeps me interested and entertained. Together, we have lots of fun."

Joy relished seeing her brother so excited since he was often very cool and level-headed. "I'm glad." She yawned. "Well, let's catch up more tomorrow. I'm beat!" She hugged her brother and bid him goodnight before retiring to her cell to rest. As soon as her head hit the pillow, she fell asleep, dreaming about Goldie, dance moves, and anxiety.

KING STING LOOKED AT his beloved with concern and admiration. Royal was gazing back, unashamed. "My love, how blessed are we?" She buzzed tenderly.

"My Queen, is there no way I can steer you away from such a dangerous task?"

Royal sighed with understanding. "Sting, the wild hive may be one of the only reasons we are free from Buzzz's ruthless leadership. If this is how I can express my gratitude to them in return, then so be it."

"Royal, let me fly beside you. I can't let you go without me."

"You won't be able to fly with me, but if you want to go to the drone congregation area, you can blend in there and keep me in your sights." Royal faltered, her voice breaking. She knew she needed to help the wild hive, but it didn't make this task any less dangerous and scary. A queen was rarely ever meant to leave her hive, since its very survival depended on her. It went against every instinct to leave. But, Royal had made up her mind after hearing Thistle's report. She would honor the wild hive and prove herself a grateful and beneficial ally. She leaned into Sting's arms for comfort. "I'd be glad for the extra security if you came."

"Anything for you, dear. Life without you would be so... dull." Sting held on to his mate. The two had grown a deep bond through their unusual story. They led the hive together, unified and honorable. Royal could never have imagined such a good thing would come from her placement in Hive Honey Quest. She was more blown away every day. Sting was a safe place for her to unload her pressures and emotions. He helped her rest. And on top of that, they had even begun bonding deeply over matters of the heart. Sting became more and more virtuous with time. She reveled in the miraculous nature of their relationship, and thanked Lighthive for it every day.

"Lighthive willing, all will be well, my love. But I'd prefer to just stay in your arms forever."

Chapter 7: Peace

Sweet Pea waited eagerly at the edge of the crowd in the landing grounds. After a packed week of training, Joy and her brother Courage would graduate from newborns to fully-fledged hive members. Pea had been honored to mentor such a brilliant and sweet young bee. She waited in her thoughts as the hive continued to gather.

The weather had changed quite a bit in the last week. The breeze was frigid, and the trees which had previously been painted in bright colors began to lose their vibrancy. Giant brown leaves fell from above. *Flowerwilt has come, and Flowersleep will be here very soon. I'm old; I will not make it past the cold season, for sure. What a life I've lived. I've gotten to taste love and freedom.* Pea was pulled away from her thoughts as Royal signaled for silence to speak.

"Good morning everyone!" She paused as the room exploded with cheers. "Today, two young bees graduate, and begin their service to the hive! Joy, Courage, stand!" Sweet Pea looked on proudly at her apprentice. Thistle, Iris, and Flower stood beside her.

Flower jumped up and down with misty eyes. "That's my Joy!"

"Joy, do you agree to dedicate your life to serving the hive and protecting your queen?"

"I do!" Joy exclaimed with passion.

Royal asked the same question of Courage. Sweet Pea noticed that Courage was more steady than his sister, and his eyes radiated with humility and strength. He also agreed to serve the hive. The two siblings stood together on the platform and the crowd roared. After the young bees took their places beside Pea and the other mentors, Royal continued.

"There is more to say. First of all, I thank all of you for your hard work here. It is nigh time to direct our best efforts into storing food throughout the hive. The Honeybandits could come at any moment now for their share of the honey, and after they do, we need to kick into high gear to prepare ourselves. We need to ensure that there will be enough food in the new comb to last through Flowersleep. Food is becoming more scarce now as flowers are aging, so you'll need to pay attention to the beedances for directions to the best sources. In addition to our physical well-being, many of you have been able to meet with a spiritual mentor. I encourage you - feel free to schedule more time if you have further questions you need answered. And those who haven't yet met with Love, Nectar, or Pollen, I strongly encourage you to do so. Another mentor will become available as well, so there should be more openings soon."

This means she will talk to Courage and appoint him. Sweet Pea thought back on the tumultuous meeting in which Nectar shared Lighthive's decision. It had definitely stirred the pot, and Hope had been very angry and hurt. *I haven't even seen the girl in ages. I hope she's doing okay.* It was definitely hard to wrap her head around Courage - a newborn - being appointed to lead others, but Pea was not about to challenge it. *Lighthive is always good, even when I don't get it.*

"There is one more thing. Today, I will be leaving the hive for a few hours." The whole crowd gasped in shock, murmuring to each other. The Queen continued. "Our allies, the Hive of Soldiers, are in need of my help tonight. I ask for a few volunteers to help on our mission. Danger is possible, but unlikely. I will go well-protected."

The whole room raised their hands in unison, including Pea. *The Queen? Leaving the hive? This is definitely a bad idea. I have to be there.*

"Courage, Thistle, and Iris, please go ahead with King Sting and a team of drones who will leave immediately. And with me, I will have..." Pea waited eagerly as Royal listed off over a hundred names. She waited to hopefully hear her own. "...and Sweet Pea. That should be enough. Gather around me so I can explain our mission. The rest of you, go enjoy some late-season nectar, or enjoy a restful evening inside before your nectar endeavors tomorrow. Thank you all."

Pea waited eagerly as the room began to clear. She wondered what this mission could be. *For the Queen to leave the hive, it must be serious. And yet, she said it wouldn't be overly dangerous.* The group of bees remaining huddled around the Queen with curiosity.

"Nectar, I need you to communicate with the doctor and caregiver bees. If I don't return by sundown, they will need to feed royal jelly to a few pupae to raise some queens. There will be no time to waste with the cold season approaching rapidly." The Queen's nurse bee nodded rigidly and set off. Everyone else tried to be patient. "Girls, fly with me. I will explain on the way."

The crowd was confused, but pressed on quietly. They filed out of the hive's entrance and created a buffer around Royal. As they exited the hive's entrance, everyone waited with anticipation as Royal took a deep breath. "Girls, we are on our way to a drone congregation area." Everyone gasped. "You all know I'm no longer searching for a mate, so be at peace. Our job is to draw the drones there as far away from the Hive of Soldiers as possible, and be a distraction. While we are gone, the wild hive will seal up its entrance in preparation for Flowersleep." She paused. "Now, this will not be a typical flight ceremony. It's your job to protect me from the drones. A few of our own drones are with them and will help to protect me as well, including King Sting."

"How should we protect you?" Sweet Pea pushed all of her more trifling questions aside as she tried to understand her job. "Do we need to fight?"

"Fighting shouldn't be necessary, because our first goal is to not get caught. I hope you girls have your racing stripes on!" Royal laughed warmly. "Speed and unpredictability is our greatest weapon. I will be changing directions constantly, and it'll be you girls' job to keep up. Now if some drones happen to catch up to us, I will need one of you to cause them to falter in flight and lose momentum. Do this even if it means some of you lose momentum too. I must have at least ten of you with me though. If you do take a drone down, gather together at the edge of Ally Forest so we can regroup before returning to the hive."

"How will we lose the drones in the end? Certainly we aren't going to be able to exhaust them." A worker asked.

"Good question! After about 20 minutes, the wild hive will be properly sealed. At my signal, we will stop in our tracks. Then, Sting will announce that I am not a new queen seeking mates, and those chasing will stop their pursuit. If anyone persists, our drones will chase them off. This mission shouldn't pose any real danger. I am of no interest to the drones congregating unless I am seeking a mate."

Sweet Pea took a deep breath as the Queen concluded. *We should all be okay... but I won't let anything happen to Queen Royal on my watch. Absolutely not.*

POLLEN WAS EXHAUSTED. After returning from the Honeycrystal a few days ago, she felt a deeper connection with Lightive. She had spent every waking hour since in meetings with countless bees. Some were acquaintances or friends, and others were strangers. Pollen was being stretched far beyond her capacity. Since there was no way to provide all the necessary and valuable mentorship from her own strength and knowledge, she was learning to rely on the Light within. And despite its unrelenting provision, she was grateful for a lighter day today with less appointments. Her aging body and mind needed the rest.

Every night, Pollen hoped she'd get to see Bravewing in her dreams. She had so much more to ask him and to learn. But he hadn't visited her again until last night. Seeing him helped her to keep going even though it was hard. She remembered what he told her. *"When you have nothing left, that forces you to realize that you need the Light. All you need to do is rest in it and let it speak through you. In those moments, what comes out of your mouth will be far superior to anything you would be capable of on your own."* Pollen understood this now. She just wasn't totally sure how to "rest in" the Light. But she knew the Light had given her words for others many times over the last days.

Pollen made it to the meeting room she was stationed in. Love and Nectar each had their own rooms next door. The bee who had booked her first appointment knocked at the door. "Come on in!"

It was the young and vibrant Joy. Pollen smiled as she entered the room. "Joy! I just watched you graduate. How are you?"

"I'm doing well!" The young worker buzzed shyly.

Pollen offered her a seat. "What questions do you have for me today?"

Joy hesitated. "Well, I really feel that I've been getting to know Lighthive little by little. I think it will continue to grow. I'm actually dealing with something else at the moment." She paused. "I... went to a small meeting in the hive recently, and I ended up leaving early. I don't know if it was my social anxiety, or if my gut was telling me something, but it felt off. How do I know if it was the Light guiding me or if it was my own mind?"

Pollen paused. "What did it feel like?"

"It felt like some sort of... imminent doom. It was small, but I still couldn't ignore it. I didn't feel like I was in danger at that very moment, but that danger could come."

Pollen took a moment to think. "Both anxiety and guidance could give you that feeling. However, anxiety often comes from your own internal fear, while guidance comes from Lighthive watching over you and protecting you. When you left the meeting, did you continue to feel conflicted and unsure? Or did you feel peace?"

Joy lit up. "I felt peace!" She looked up at Pollen. "Do you think that means I made the right decision?"

"I can't be certain of course, but I know that whenever I make the right decision, it's followed by peace. Peace, big or small, comes from the Light. And if I ever made the wrong decision, I felt other things. Things like doubt, unease, and a need to justify myself. I could become confident in my wrong choice, but there was always something nagging me about it. That's the Light." She took a breath. "Peace isn't just feeling comfortable. It's a feeling that your conscience is clear. It is an underlying faith that all is well and you are in good hands, no matter how crazy your life feels above it all."

Joy sighed. "Thanks Pollen! I think I made the right decision. I can apply what you've said in the future. Peace versus unease. That's good." Her brow scrunched. "There's something else that's been weighing on me though. Whatever that group is, it made me feel unsettled. And I recognized someone else there."

Pollen tilted her head. "If you are concerned, I can look into it for you. Who did you recognize?"

"It was Hope."

Chapter 8: A Surprise Visiter

The hive waited in uncomfortable anticipation without their Queen. Inner turmoil was natural for any bee who's Queen might be in danger, and many workers filled the landing grounds, pacing anxiously. Murmurs erupted everywhere like, *"She ought to be back any moment now!"*, *"I hope everything is ok..."*, and *"What if she's hurt?"*. The sun outside was setting and a chill blew into the hive as the cold season loomed.

Suddenly and with great force, Royal and scores of other bees erupted into the grounds. The crowd exploded with gasps and cheers. Royal stopped, breathlessly hovering above them all. "The HoneyBandits approach as we speak. Hunker down!"

Hysteria ensued as bees scrambled in every direction. Their Queen had returned safely, but now the HoneyBandits were coming. Some of them rushed the Queen to the back of the hive to find safety in the throne room. Nothing could happen to her.

The ground began to rumble just a bit. The movement became more and more intense as the big creature approached. At first, the bees kept themselves from swarming. But then, the whole hive shook as a blinding light washed over them. The HoneyBandit had arrived, and had removed the roof of their home. At this point, the hive really panicked. Bees began to swarm, terrified. Billows of smoke coursed through the hive, driving many of the remaining bees to evacuate. This smoke also suppressed their warning signals, causing mass confusion.

The creature began removing rows of comb, and slowly, a massive void in the hive grew and grew. It continued removing frames for some time, and the minutes felt long. When the Honeybandit had finished, only four or five frames of honey remained, including the nursery. A few bees had even been crushed in the process. A couple of fresh, empty frames were slid into the hive, but there was still a great emptiness. Then, the ceiling was replaced with a low rumble. Almost as suddenly as it began, it was over.

It took the hive a long time to regroup. Some bees swarmed in terror outside for a while before returning to their nearly unrecognizable home and its eery vastness. Everything was silent for several minutes as they recovered from the emotional whiplash of today. After it was certainly over and the HoneyBandit would not return, Royal was retrieved from the throne room. She gathered them all in the new void. "Tend to any wounded, and everyone else should go pollinate. We will fill as much of the new comb as we can. Before long, the cold will force us to close the hive entrance." Everyone went to work without hesitation, allowing their adrenaline to fuel them.

Courage had returned with Royal and everyone else. Their mission had been successful, and none of them were hurt. The hive was seemingly relieved that their Queen was home safely. Courage was exhausted and drained though after the mission - having flown more than he ever had before in one day. *I don't care if it's early... I need sleep.* He trudged to his cell, hardly acknowledging the disheveled hive. *I can get to my cell more easily now... but so many areas have been destroyed.* As he almost reached the edge of the clearing, someone stopped him. He turned to see his mother, Royal.

"Your Majesty!" He bowed his head instinctually. "What do you need?"

The Queen looked at him with wonder. "My son. I need to deliver Lighthive's message." She paused, a peculiar expression on her face. "You have been chosen to mentor within the hive. Lighthive had selected Nectar, Pollen, Love, and you."

Courage was completely shocked. "I... am so young and new. What can I teach anyone else?"

Royal tilted her head. "To be frank, your appointment was a surprise to all of us. However, we trust in Lighthive even when it seems to go against all reason. You bear an old soul Courage. I have faith that you will contribute greatly to this hive. I've known since the day you were born."

Courage lowered his gaze, his thoughts spinning. "When would I begin?"

"Take a day to rest and meditate. Then on the following day, go to the Honeycrystal when the sun is at its peak. It may be your only chance before it's too cold. You'll begin your role as a mentor the day after your trip." She touched her dear son's shoulder. "Let Lighthive be what you cannot. Thanks for all of your help today. Go and get some rest." The Queen smiled before turning away to tend to her hive.

Me??? Courage was completely baffled. Shaking his head in bewilderment, he trudged to his cell. He sat on his pollen-stuffed cushion and stared blankly at the wall. *I literally know nothing of Lighthive.*

Of course you do.

Courage perked up, scanning the room for the voice. No one was to be found.

Come on, man! Focus! It has been quite long enough that we've had to ignore you to allow for your focused training. There is no more time. You know that turmoil is at hand! Why haven't you done anything to prepare, River?

"Who are you?" Courage buzzed quietly, sitting upright and alert. He wasn't sure why, but hearing this random voice coming from nowhere didn't terrify him. It sounded familiar. A sense of safety resided within him, and something else too - he felt a deep curiosity that couldn't be quenched. "And my name is Courage."

Don't tell me you've remembered nothing! It's me, Forest! And you are Courageous River, yes. Sky, Meadow, and I have been so patient but the time for patience is over! You must meet with us tonight!

Courage paused, soaking in that name. It felt so true. "How?" He asked, his head spinning trying to process this moment. It was as if his subconscious was comfortable and at ease, and yet he couldn't access that part of himself to understand it. There was a deep, foreign mass within him he couldn't identify.

Oh my, it's worse than I thought. Through your dreams, River. Your dreams. Hurry up!

Then, the voice was gone. Courage stayed still for a few minutes, clawing at the secrets within himself for answers. It was to no avail. He didn't understand what was happening, but he was filled with a feeling of peace and knowing about it nonetheless. Part of him was nervous to fall asleep, but another part of him was filled with longing. Longing to know this part of himself he was sensing, and longing to talk to this bee. He stirred out of his stupor so he could quickly complete his bedtime routine. After his final chore, he lowered himself onto his cushion. It took forever to wind down since his mind was racing with questions and curiosities. But after about an hour, he finally fell into a trance-like sleep.

It felt like the exact moment his subconsciousness kicked in, he was waking up. *Huh?* Courage felt disoriented as he looked around. *Am I dreaming? Or is this real?* He was standing on the floor of a grandiose forest. It looked as if it was golden hour, and ethereal rays peeked through the wood. Slowly, his sense of hearing was restored.

"River? River, wake up!" It was Forest's voice, except it was right beside him this time instead of in his head.

Courage looked over at him, blinking in wonder. He recognized this drone somehow, and tried to piece together shards of the memories that were coming to him. But they were only fragments. "Wow, I feel weird."

Forest rolled his eyes. "I don't have the patience for this right now."

"River, is it you?" A sweet, flowery voice rang across the mossy expanse.

"Meadow?" Courage jumped at his own voice when calling out that name. *Meadow...* His heart began to flutter and his face grew warm. He turned to see two elegant queen bees flying toward him rapidly. Squinting, Courage tried to remember more. His memories felt barely out of grasp. As they reached the place where he stood, one landed beside Forest and the other approached him meekly.

Sky spoke up first. "I'm sorry we ran late. We were consulting some of the others."

"No worries." The gruff drone visibly softened with Sky at his side.

Meadow smiled up at Courage warmly, tears in her eyes. "Oh, how I've missed you."

"How much do you remember?" Sky asked.

"Not much... only that I feel like I've known you all once." Courage mumbled.

Sky sighed with understanding. "River, we warned you about this before you decided to go. The effects of leaving can lead to total amnesia about your past life. But with a little work, I think we can help you restore it."

"No matter what we said to dissuade you, nothing would get in the way of you helping Hive Honey Quest." Meadow looked at him admiringly. She held herself back from embracing him.

Courage returned her gaze. Emotions flooded within him. He could sense her affection toward him, and his toward her. "Tell me more."

Sky interjected quietly. "Forest and I will be near the Hive of Souls." She winked before the two flew off, leaving Courage and Meadow alone together.

"So.." Meadow began, "what do they call you?"

"I'm called Courage." He watched her take a step closer to him. A deep love for her was ever present within him. He was filled with admiration, respect, affection, honor, warmth, and desire. It was such a strange situation. He wasn't sure if he could take her into his arms, but that's all he wanted to do.

"That is the perfect name for you." Meadow smiled. "You must have so many questions."

"All I seem to remember is you." Courage drew closer.

Meadow blushed. She gestured to a patch of particularly soft moss. As soon as Courage sat down, she sat beside him and took his hand. They reveled in each other's presence for a moment, enjoying the closeness. Meadow shed a few more tears, looking up at him. "Oh, how I've missed you." Several more moments passed before she straightened up and sat across from him to look at his face. "I could stay here forever. But we do have a time limit. At some point, you will have to wake up." She wiped her face dry. "Ask me anything. I will fill in the gaps of your memory until it feels like your own again."

"Tell me the story of how I ended up in Hive Honey Quest." Courage wanted to swim in the sound of her voice.

"Well, we sensed trouble ahead, while less so in a physical sense. There's a turmoil growing within the heart of the hive. After The War of the Ghost, we were filled with joy at the potential of winning back the hive and its loyalty like old days, but this inner turmoil has the ability to risk it all and spoil this chance. We all decided that we should send someone to help the situation, because matters of the heart are of the utmost importance. Hive Honey Quest was once our home and is now filled with our descendants." She paused, blushing.

"*Our* descendants?" Courage asked, smiling.

"Yes. You have always been an honorable King, and were very quick to volunteer to go. We agreed that you would have a good chance of handling the transition well to be able to help the hive. But since this is rarely done, we weren't sure what might happen. We watched over Royal through her painful delivery, helping in any way we could. There was some resistance for your re-entrance into the world. Thank Lighthive you made it. Royal's faith made it possible." She sighed. "And we've been waiting patiently since your hatching to wake you up to your purpose. We wanted to do so at the right moment."

"What is my purpose?" Courage buzzed.

"You are to help our descendents thrive once again. They will thrive within, which is true prosperity. They will be restored."

Courage pondered this for a moment. It was heavy. He wasn't sure how he'd help heal the inner turmoil in Hive Honey Quest, but his appointment to mentor the hive made a lot more sense now. It would certainly be one way to reach their hearts. He chose to ask something to satisfy his curiosities next. "Who are some of our direct descendents?"

Meadow perked up. "There are far too many to name. But I can list some. Sting, Pollen," Meadow hesitated, "even Buzzz."

Courage winced at the name of the hive's long lost enemy. *I wonder where he is now. Is he dead, or still alive? Will he come back?*

"River, our time is coming to an end." The sweet Queen looked sad.

"Can I see you again in my dreams? I know that this... this is my real world. I feel so incredibly at home. But I have to complete the task at hand. I won't quit until I have played out my purpose." He touched Meadow's hand. "But I have to see you as much as possible. I have so much to learn, and I already miss you dearly." This time, it was his turn to get misty eyed.

"Of course. Now that the barrier has been broken down, you can visit any time. Don't worry, you will still always wake up rested and fulfilled. And as for your purpose, it will be made clear to you when the timing is right. Start by remembering your connection to Lighthive so you can mentor our descendants." Meadow's voice began to sound further away. She touched his face and looked into his eyes. Just before he slipped away, she gave him a tender kiss.

Chapter 9: The Monarch

Hope was quiet amidst the hustle and bustle of visiting around her. *Finally I've found a place where I belong, bees who see my value... and a way to find happiness.* Hope had been attending every New Beginning meeting since her first. Everyone had accepted her with open arms, and for once, she felt good. She felt safe, relaxed, and appreciated. She was having fun again.

Hope hadn't fully realized just how intense her life had been since day one until she was given the opportunity to unwind. She'd had time to really reflect on it all, and that deep anger she carried grew. How was it fine for Lighthive to have destined her with such a heavy burden, and yet not trust her with anything or allow her any credit for the overcoming of her trials? It felt good to work through these feelings and identify why she was so upset and wronged.

As she reflected, the crowd around Hope grew silent, and she looked up at the stage to see Goldie preparing to speak.

"Welcome everyone! Today is a special day. Firstly, you will get to meet our leader. You all know her name to be Sun. However, you must refer to her as The Monarch. She runs things here. She's the reason that all of you are finally home." Goldie paused dramatically as the crowd cheered. "Secondly, we've been growing quickly! All of you who have joined us are family. The Monarch sees fit that a few of you will be selected to take positions of leadership within the group."

The crowd buzzed with excitement and sudden anticipation. Who would be selected to help lead?

"Before that though, I want to remind you all that your loyalty is of the utmost importance. There are many forces looking to work against us. Some bees can't bear to allow others to experience happiness, or to live their lives as they please. Remember that if anyone is against you, they are against us. We must protect our right to live our lives. If anyone opposes your involvement in this group, they are not a friend to you. They want you to join in their misery. Such is the nature of most bees. But you are all special. We have chosen you carefully amidst the hive because you are different. You have something to offer. You deserve happiness. Remember that if you find someone else like you and me, they also deserve to be a part of the family. You should reach out and offer this gift to them as well."

The members cheered with approval as Goldie stepped down. Anticipation bubbled as they waited for The Monarch. The moments felt like minutes.

Hope was standing next to Theo. She had been friends with Theo's brother Thistle before, but had drifted apart recently. Theo had joined the New Beginning almost immediately after the war, clearly seeking something tangible to apply himself to. Hope had run into him quite often since.

He seemed to like it there, but he was always restless as if he wanted more. He had been Buzzz's right hand man, after all. He clearly craved to hold a position of importance again. "Have you met The Monarch before?" Hope offered as they waited.

Theo grunted. "A time or two." He was not often much of a chatter. "Honestly, I'm not much for these fancy meetings. I just come along to appease them." He let out a coarse chuckle.

Hope laughed too. Suddenly, the nervous chatter of the crowd died down. Not a sound could be heard besides the slow steps of an ascending worker bee. Soon, Sun came into view. Small gasps were heard as the crowd beheld her and her grandiose attire. She wore a piece from a monarch butterfly wing as a cape, held on by delicate strands from vines and ferns. The cape's colors had somehow been vividly preserved as if the wing was still attached to its original owner. She looked absolutely marvelous.

Sun approached the podium with grace, and lifted her voice. "What a joy to see you all today!" She clapped her hands to encourage applause. Her voice was rich, commanding, and dynamic. With just a single sentence, it was clear that everybee was paying attention.

After the clapping, she continued with a long-winded speech. "At New Beginning, our mission is to pursue self-improvement and happiness! You all have chosen your home in this hive, and it is here. I am honored to lead us toward that goal." Sun paused. "Today, you will be assigned your first tasks. Each and every one of you must deliver a load of honey to our private stores before the next meeting. We all must work toward the common goal. Anyone who doesn't deliver is not a true member, and will not be welcome. Show me how dedicated you are to this family. There will be other tasks soon, as we continue developing as a group. This is your chance to rise above your fellow members. Those who go above and beyond for New Beginning will be rewarded. Speaking of that, today I will appoint a few of you to oversee these tasks and lead smaller subgroups. Those three will be members of my entourage and will be versed in the plans I have for us all." She took a long moment before proceeding, building anticipation in the crowd. Then, she slowly called out two names that Hope didn't recognize, followed by: "...and Hope. You three have shown excellent zeal and leadership skills. Please come with me now." With that, The Monarch bowed before the crowd and descended from the stage. Everyone cheered.

Hope was in shock. *Me?* Hearing her name had surprised her so much that it took her several moments to fully register it. Beside her, Theo hissed in frustration, hardly even looking at Hope before buzzing off. *I hope he's okay...* She didn't dwell on a concern for him though. Hope had been waiting for someone to see her worth. Her chest swelled with pride as she fully realized the honor of such a position, letting it really sink in. She parted through the crowd toward the back of the stage. *I have been waiting to be seen. To be valued. And now*

I am. Hope was glowing. When she had first been born, power and responsibility daunted her. But after she had fulfilled her tasks, it seemed like everybee forgot what she had done. She wasn't celebrated as a key soldier. No one even thanked her. Ever since defeating Buzzz, she longed for that powerful purpose again - to be needed and wanted. She knew she was capable of big things.

Two other bees stood with her, one a drone and the other a worker. She glanced at them to smile. The she-bee hardly half-smiled back, carrying herself with arrogance. The drone looked tough. He smiled back at her. "Aye, whattya know?"

The three turned to see The Monarch emerge from a shadow. "Welcome. Congratulations on your promotions. You've all exhibited great ambition and resolve. Join me for a meeting with my entourage. Be prepared to learn a lot more about our family." She began to lead them away when she paused seriously. "This is your last chance to walk away. Know that once we enter those doors, your life will be for New Beginning and our cause. By accepting your promotion, you make a commitment. Leaving is not an option."

Deep down Hope was a bit shaken by Sun's sudden intensity, but her surprise was overshadowed by a deep loyalty within. She and the two others nodded solemnly, and they followed Sun into the meeting space.

The energy in the room was different. It was intense. But, Hope enjoyed it. *I'm finally important. I will do anything to prove I'm worthy!* The three newbies took their places in empty chairs. Five or so other bees, most older and wiser, eyed the newcomers warily.

"Have they sworn their loyalty?" One worker asked loudly.

"Yes, they have." Sun responded.

A very old drone peered at Hope and her fellow recruits. "Well, we shouldn't be wasting our time then. Let's get a move on." His gruff voice bellowed.

Sun folded her hands after seating herself at the head of the table. Even though she was surrounded by her council, it was clear that she was the most powerful member by miles. She composed herself for a long speech. "Newcomers and elders, let us review the plans for New Beginning within the hive, especially in regards to the cold season upon us. Reserve all questions until you are told. We have a large amount of personal stores of honey. Flowersleep is coming early this year, and is expected to be a rough one. Once the hive is sealed, we will eat from community honey stores until they are low. Then, we will take what we need from our personal stores to remain strong, without allowing ourselves to appear overly fed. As the hive deals with crises, we will seem to be sharing in their struggles. The hive will reach a low point where it is vulnerable. When the time is just right, we will assume leadership of the hive. This is the very shortest version, but I can answer your questions now."

Hope tried to conceal the shock on her face. During her moment of bewilderment, the other appointed she-bee, a sharp and quick-thinking worker, raised her hand. "First of all, this hive will not submit easily to "assumed" leadership. Are you insinuating that there may be war?"

Sun smiled. "Any who resist will be dispatched."

Hope's throat was dry as she spoke next to respond to this. "What does that mean for Royal?"

"There is no room for two queens" The Monarch retorted dryly.

"Will we raise a queen from her offspring?" Hope tried to conceal her wavering voice with a confident expression.

"Absolutely not. We already have one."

The three recruits looked around in confusion. "Who?" The drone chuckled uneasily.

Sun's face became angry. "You stand before her now. I am a laying worker." Hope gasped. Laying workers were pretty uncommon - about one in every hundred. They rarely ever laid eggs and were very limited compared to a queen's capabilities. They were only capable of laying unfertilized eggs which grew into drones. Therefore, a laying worker could never raise a new queen or keep up with the demands of a hive.

Hope spoke again before thinking, caught up in the logic of her thought process. "A hive needs more than a few drones. How will we be able to sustain it?"

Sun's eyes flashed. She was both furious and oddly pleased. "I am not just any laying worker. I am capable." Her eye contact was brazen, and Hope realized the possible disrespect of her retort.

The room was silent for a moment before Sun continued. "I am a Thelytoky."

Chapter 10: Reconciliation

Thelytoky? What is that? Hope waited nervously with wide eyes as Sun began to explain.

"A Thelytoky is able to produce male AND female offspring. I don't even need a drone to do it." Sun shook her wings with pride. "There is nothing stopping me from raising a queen."

Hope paused for a moment with curiosity and wonder. "Has this ever been done before? Will it really be possible?"

Sun stared at her with annoyance. "Thelytoky bees have existed before. They have produced workers before. There is no reason raising a queen would not be possible." It seemed Hope had struck a sensitive cord in her, revealing a shred of doubt in her guarded eyes.

After letting it sink in for a moment, Hope realized what this all meant. Her very own mother and likely many of her sisters and brothers would be killed according to this plan. *Is it worth it?* Only moments before, she had known nothing of this. She had found a sense of belonging and appreciation in this group. But that was all she thought it to be. She didn't know the group had a vision to overthrow her mother and assume ownership of the hive. It all seemed much more sinister than she had originally realized.

The Monarch interrupted her thoughts. "My expectations on the three of you new leaders are very high. You must NEVER miss a gathering. You will also have extra meetings with our team of leaders to discuss our plans and goals. You will play key roles in how all of this unfolds. Take pride in your position, and try to recruit as many bees as you can. Remember, recruiting involves helping each bee see why the group would benefit their lives. Appeal to their egos. Offer them a community. Soon, we will need to stop recruiting if we want to take the hive. We need a unified front of strong-minded followers - not scattered. Build incentive for members to become more involved and dedicated. If anyone doesn't fit our mold, they will need to be kicked out. We can't risk having a traitor in our midst."

Hope blinked. Glancing at the other new leaders, she saw their eyes sparkling with ambition and zeal. She took care to appear as on-board as possible. *I have a feeling trying to leave now could actually cost me my life. But I don't know about all of this.*

After a few more minutes, they were wrapping up. "To a New Beginning!" The room cheered, and the meeting commenced. Hope left the room last. The hall where everyone had gathered was eerily empty, leaving her alone with a mess of thoughts. She really would have rather run away, but she couldn't. New Beginning's plans were blatant and clear. They would kill anyone in their way, including Queen Royal. She couldn't fathom how this had been the undertone all along, and she'd had not the slightest idea.

Hope struggled. She had held deep resentment against her closest family members and her mother. She had lost her trust in Lighthive, which they all held as their first priority, even over her. Hope had led a complicated life filled with expectations, emotions, and lack of appreciation. New Beginning had given her a sense of purpose within her darkness. It had made her feel affirmed, safe, and free. But in this moment, she felt more trapped than ever. *If I leave, I'll probably be killed. But if I stay, others will die. And I will have played a key role in it.*

What are you going to do?

Hope grimaced as she heard Lightwing's sweet voice in her subconscious. "Well this really bites." She said aloud. "I'm so angry with you."

What have I done?

"Why have I been subject to such an existence? I'd rather not have tasted life at all." Hope kicked the ground. "There is so little comfort and goodness here. I can barely catch my breath."

All we have ever done is offer you the truest form of peace amidst the struggle of life.

Hope shook her head. "How have you ever offered me peace?"

Living with a clear conscience, focused on the Light? There is no other way of living that gives you all you are looking for. You are heavy now with a guilty heart. You are held fast by resentment and entitlement. Do you think Lighthive offers a life free from any trial?

"Apparently not."

The Light offers an eternal haven even amidst the imperfections of this world. It offers peace, purpose, and an overflowing of love from an endless source. It rejects selfishness and the desire to control your own life. It promises an unwavering help through anything that comes your way. It makes the impossible possible.... You must do what you know is right.

Hope squeezed her eyes shut, hot tears falling down her cheeks. "It hurts to be humiliated." She sighed, beginning to crumble. "How could I be so blind? This group was always off. I just didn't want to believe it. I just wanted to feel good again."

The greatest rest is in the Light. You can be vulnerable there. Loved. And free from chains.

Hope fell to her knees, burying her head in her arms. "Why do I always mess up?" Every emotion gripped her heart, and she couldn't even stand. Her body trembled as her mind spun.

You are loved. And, there is a way you can remedy this.

Several moments passed as Hope processed everything. Rising to her feet, she wiped away her tears and cleared her head with determination. "You're right, there is." *I was wrong. But it's not too late to make this better.*

"Excuse me? Who's there?" One of the older New Beginning leaders stepped out into the opening.

Hope jumped. "I'm sorry, I'm just thinking out loud!"

The member stared at her through squinted eyes. "You need to get out of here and get to work. Your life is for the New Beginning's purpose now. Stop dawdling!"

"Of course! My mistake!" Hope dipped her head before flying out of the room. She sighed in relief. She could have easily been overheard. *I know what I can do... what I have to do.*

POLLEN, SWEET PEA, Joy, and Hope sat together in a cell. They waited quietly and patiently for Royal and Nectar. The tension in the air was thick. No one had seen or talked to Hope in so long. Now, here she was, calling a meeting with hive leadership. Pea was Hope's closest friend, and Joy just happened to be in session with Pollen at the time, so she came along. After a few more agonizing minutes of suppressed curiosities, the doors finally opened. The Queen and her nurse bee filed in, their faces engaged with interest.

"My daughter." Queen Royal smiled at Hope widely. "I've missed you."

Hope shifted uncomfortably. "Thanks for being here. I know you're busy."

Pea stood by Hope, waiting in anticipation. Even though she was a closer friend, she knew nothing about what Hope would share. Each bee found themselves a place to sit after Hope gestured for them to get comfortable.

"I want to start by saying it has been... a tough time for me recently. I have shut the doors on you all for weeks. And I'm sorry. I've been holding anger and allowing it to guide my steps." Hope looked at all of them meaningfully, actively fighting her shame and awkwardness as she spoke slowly. Her eyes began to mist. "I have to share something very very important with you all. It's the only way I can redeem my selfish actions."

The gathering waited patiently. They looked upon Hope with shock and admiration for her admission of wrongdoing, and burning anticipation to discover what she had done.

"There are members of this hive planning terrible things against us, and against our Queen."

Chapter 11: Deeper Connections

Courage opened his eyes with excitement. Two nights ago he had reconnected with Lighthive and had been awakened to his purpose. Yesterday night, he got to spend more time with Meadow. But this sleep session yielded nothing, and he found himself peering up at his ceiling instead of tree branches. He let out a sigh. *All I want to do is see you.* He gathered himself. *But today, I will visit the Honeycrystal. I will see you then.*

He took very little time to prepare himself before departing from his room and making his way to the hive entrance. After his trip to the crystal today, Courage would begin his role providing regular mentorship. Things were going to change fast. He needed all the divine time he could get, and he wasn't going to waste a moment.

Courage was in some ways nervous, but he had a deep confidence that surprised him. He knew he'd be able to do anything with Lighthive's help. *I need to remember that this is my life right now, and reuniting with Meadow forever has to wait... even though I'd rather do nothing else than be in her presence.* After erupting from the hive entrance with vigor, he sprinted through the morning mist straight to his destination. As he flew, he meditated on some of his favorite memories from those two precious visits with Meadow.

"River, you always led our hive with such incredible wisdom. You were fiercely protective, just, kind, and never hesitant to face your fears when necessary. And you always took excellent care of your Queen." She had said, giving him a warm look as she moved closer.

Another time, she had been resting her head on him. Overtaken with emotion, she had turned to him, her gaze intense. She leaned close to his face and their antennae entwined. Tears had escaped her eyes. *"I miss you, my dear. Every moment without you is a great challenge. We are one, you know. How can one be in two places? Oh how I long for our reunion."*

Seeing Meadow was almost intoxicating. It was as if all in the world was well. But deep down, Courage knew he needed to be careful. He needed to stay focused on his purpose here, and he'd be reunited with her very soon. Still, he welcomed every moment she gave him.

"You will remember your wisdom and great leadership when it is time. And when you come home, any memories lost will be restored. But you are there for a reason, River. You must reject any urge to remain comfortable and at ease. The sooner your purpose is fulfilled, the sooner we can be together. You will help the hive find their inner compass. They will find peace and truth. You will help protect them from Darkhive."

"Darkhive?"

"Darkness is the opposite of light. While a shadow has no hope in the Light's rays, it can be tended to in secret where it thrives. Its true goal is to isolate one away from the Light. And when it succeeds, it takes control."

"Why haven't we heard of this in Hive Honey Quest?" Courage had asked.

"Usually there is no benefit to meditating on things like this. We are to focus on the Light, not darkness. But when inner war is at hand, we must acknowledge that darkness is at play. We need to defend against its attacks and protect one another. Still, keeping focused on the Light is crucial. No battle can be won by us alone."

Courage blinked, returning his consciousness to his body. To his amazement, he was already at the mouth of the Honeycrystal's network of tunnels. His mind had been thoroughly occupied for more than an hour. With vigor, he chose the correct tunnels to find the crystal. They were very dim, as the sun still had to ascend for a bit before it would hover over the cave. His journey had felt so natural and familiar, like he'd visited before.

When he reached the room, he waited for a while. Time was different in there - one moment may have actually been an hour. He sat quietly, closing his eyes and calming his mind. Then, a warmth exuded around him. He wordlessly approached the lit stone and rested on it as he slipped into a trance.

Courage was being pelted by wind as he found himself freefalling from the sky. Despite his instinctual efforts, he couldn't seem to make his wings work properly. Swiveling his head around stiffly, he saw nothing but more sky. A chill rippled through his freezing body. *If I am with Lighthive, I must be safe. I need to trust.* He relaxed his muscles and released control as he plummeted.

A few moments later, his body began tingling with warmth, and he rapidly approached the earth. He slowly twitched his wings, careful to not let them get battered by the force of the wind. Just then, a drone joined him in the sky. "Come on, River! Follow me!" Courage saw that it was Forest. The drone had whizzed past him, flying at an altitude no bee on earth would choose to attempt. Mustering all of his energy, Courage carefully used his wings to decelerate and gain control in flight. It took a great effort before he was able to finally follow his old friend.

Forest did not relent. Courage could hardly see him but was gaining on him slowly. After quite the chase, he caught up, panting with effort. Forest side-eyed him humorously. "Now what do we have here? The sky has produced a valiant roughian." He rammed into Courage playfully. Courage was pleasantly surprised by his lighter mood compared to his last run-in with him. A deep appreciation and bond with a long-lost friend burned within him.

"Forest, were we close during our lifetimes?"

Forest grunted. "I suppose you could say so. We are hilariously different, but an excellent team."

"Tell me more." Courage pressed.

His friend rolled his eyes as they coasted downward. "You and Meadow led Hive Honey Quest long ago. Sky was Meadow's sister, another Queen who had been raised for the Queen games when their mother grew old. When Meadow won leadership, Sky and I went to build our own hive not far away. A hive you know well."

Courage was surprised. "The Hive of Soldiers?"

"Bingo!" Forest grinned. "We were very amicable for years before the hives drifted and became strangers. But now, we are reconnected by a new alliance. This is a good thing."

"Wow! Amazing!" Courage smiled widely. "I had no idea!" He paused for a moment. "Does that mean Sir Taves..."

"My grandson. Great great great... great great something or other." Forest swelled with pride.

"Wow man!"

At last, the two drones approached the forest floor in the grand ravine. They landed a bit clumsily and took a few moments to recover from the exhilarating flight. Despite the ripping winds, their wings did not ache. Courage glanced up at the sky where he had fallen from in wonder. The place was vast and beautiful, and it was familiar. It had the same feeling as his dreams, but just from a different perspective. He wasn't as deep into the heart of the forest, which was perfectly lit by glorious rays of sunlight. "It's beautiful here." He took it all in. "Hey, how does visiting the Honeycrystal vary from meeting you in my dreams?"

Forest looked at Courage oddly. "Coming to the Honeycrystal is a way for you to call upon us. Dreams are a way for us to call upon you. Though there are really no rules on it, and we can connect whenever and however we please with you. But sometimes it's hard to connect with Lighthive when you live in the world. Places like the Honeycrystal can become an excellent tool." He chuckled. "Honestly, it's odd to be the one teaching you about these things. You always were the one who knew more during our lifetimes."

Courage soaked it in. "Will I get to see Meadow today?"

Forest looked serious. "I think we can both agree that seeing Meadow needs to remain less frequent right now. Your purpose on earth needs to come first."

Courage knew Forest was right, even though it pained him to admit so. He nodded curtly. "Then what am I to learn today?"

"We have plenty to discuss." Forest proceeded.

JOY LET OUT A LONG sigh. She had been a part of a big meeting this morning, but only for a few minutes. Hope had shared a lot of information. *I can't believe I almost became a part of New Beginning. It could have been me delivering bad news!* Nonetheless, her admiration for Hope was restored. The she-bee had chosen to act before it was too late, despite knowing that she was risking her life. Hope could be saving the entire hive from this group's dark plans. She shared more after Joy had been dismissed from the meeting, and while she burned with curiosity, she knew that some things were meant to remain in the hands of leadership.

The day of questions and queries had dragged on, and now Joy was resting in her room. She recalled how she'd felt uneasy about New Beginning straight away. This was a powerful moment for her, since she now knew her inklings had been correct. She'd know for any future scenarios what it feels like when Lighthive sends a warning. It solidified things for her.

Interrupting her thoughts, she heard the door close in the cell next to her. *Courage!* Joy hadn't connected with her dear brother in so long, and she missed him terribly. She immediately went to knock.

"Who is it?"

"It's Joy."

"Come in." Joy entered his cell, happy to see him. She peered at him as he lay on his pollen stuffed cushion, clearly exhausted. While he looked tired, his eyes gleamed with warmth and passion as he stared at his ceiling. It was as if he weren't totally present.

"I've missed you, brother." Joy sat herself beside him. "You seem... Well, you're a walking contradiction aren't you?" She looked down at him with amusement. "You look as though you have not a shred of effort left in your body, and yet... your gaze is alight with energy!"

Courage blinked obliviously as he looked at his sister. "I don't know what you mean." His eyes were glazed over like he was living in another reality. Shaking his head, he yawned. "I've been learning a lot. Maybe you are seeing the fire of knowledge in me." He chuckled, at last becoming fully present. "How are you sister?"

Joy smiled curiously. "I'm alright. It's been a very eventful few days. I was just in a meeting with hive leadership this morning. There are some internal concerns in the hive I have learned a bit about."

Courage tilted his head with piqued interest. "Tell me more."

Joy did her best to summarize what she knew. She reminded him about her personal experience with New Beginning, and then detailed how Hope had made leadership aware of a threat. After about ten minutes, she concluded. "I know I was only given the short story before I was asked to leave, and I too have plenty of unanswered questions. Honestly, it was by pure chance that I even got to know this much, since I was scheduled with Pollen when she was summoned. Because I happened to have experienced New Beginning, she let me tag along. But Queen Royal plans to remain quiet for the time being while a plan is formulated."

Courage looked deeply thoughtful. "We are very lucky to know about this so far in advance. I will need to see how I can help." He paused, looking at Joy. "Tomorrow, I will begin as a mentor for the hive."

Joy gasped, bewildered. "What? I've definitely missed something here!"

He caught her up on his conversation with the Queen two days ago, and how Lighthive had selected him. "Honestly, I had no idea why I was chosen, and I felt very unequipped."

Joy studied him. "But not anymore?"

"Well…" Courage looked a bit guarded as she probed. "I visited the Honeycrystal today. And it's safe to say a lot has changed for me in the last few days. Lighthive has definitely been revealing itself to me in a huge way. I honestly feel like a completely different drone."

"Wow." Joy had so many questions. "What was it like? The Honeycrystal, I mean, and your visit?"

"I honestly couldn't summarize it in an hour. Really, I'm just learning so much."

"Well, don't forget about us little guys while you're mentoring, and hanging out with your messenger!" Joy laughed. She saw Courage's face change again. He looked wistful and far away. His face softened, and his cheeks filled with warmth. "Courage, is there something else you need to tell me? I've never seen you quite so… distracted." Then, a crazy thought came to her. "Have you met someone?"

Courage turned red. "What? Why would you say that?"

Joy got excited. "Bro! How have I not heard about this yet? You have much to tell!"

"I, well, it's kind of difficult to explain!" The drone's expression was filled with emotion. "I mean, yeah. I suppose I have met someone." Joy stared at him expectantly. "A lovely Queen. She's… everything anyone could want."

"Well, when did you meet her?" Joy was exploding with questions.

"A few days ago. She's… not from around here." Courage spoke cautiously. "Her name is Meadow. It's strange. In one sense, I just met her. But in a way, part of me feels like I've known her forever. She's beautiful, wise, supportive, kind, and warm." He was gleaming. "And I think she loves me."

"Courage! This is huge!" Joy was bubbling over, when she hesitated. "Wait, does this mean you'll be leaving the hive?" *I don't know how I'd fare without him...*

Courage paused. "No, not yet. But maybe in the future. Trust me sister, if I ever do leave, I'll be sure to visit often." He looked at his sister meaningfully. "But for now I'm not going anywhere, except maybe to dreamland!" He glanced down wistfully at his soft pillow and yawned.

Joy nodded with amusement as she stood up to leave. "Well, have a great sleep brother. If you can." She winked before she left. *I can't believe it! My brother's in love!*

Chapter 12: Parting Ceremony

Royal was troubled. There was a lot on her mind, as usual, and the pace of life felt especially fast. It had been a few days now since she had successfully helped the wild hive with a small favor, and she knew that soon, Hive Honey Quest would also be sealed off. It would be any day now with the impending cold. Countless bees had been devoted to harvesting the ever-scarcer nectar to pack as much as possible away, but quantities were still considerably lower than ideal for such an early approaching frost, despite her planning. She now knew that part of this had to do with New Beginning's personal staching reported by Hope.

Royal knew that the hive wouldn't be safe while New Beginning was there, and yet she knew now was not the time to act. She would have to coexist until the right moment came. All the while, she'd need to watch her back, and do everything she could to protect Hope as well.

Another thing weighed on her. It was customary that before the hive would be sealed, there'd be a parting ceremony. Many bees who were old would voluntarily partake, and ultimately would never return. They would take a final flight just before dusk, and find a late-season flower to sip on until the cold of night swept in on them.

Death was a normal part of the cycle in a hive. Many lives were short. But this time, Royal knew she'd be parting with her daughters. Love, Trust, Peace, Faith, and even her dear friend Pollen had signed their names to participate, among many others. The Queen's heart hurt, knowing she'd be saying goodbye to some of her dearest hive members. The parting ceremony would take place this very night.

The Queen sat in vigil beside her little nurse bee, Nectar, and King Sting. She rested her head on Sting's shoulder for comfort as a tear escaped her eye. "Life will not be the same." She spoke feebly. "Every day I create life, and for years I have seen those lives reach their end. It becomes difficult to bear, especially now."

Sting buried his face into his mate's fur. "You are so strong. And I am here for you." He held her close.

Nectar hummed a quiet, mournful melody. Its enchanting notes were filled with sorrow, and yet laced with a powerful peace. The King and Queen closed their eyes to listen intently.

A soul must go on as her mortal life ends,
Sail to the beyond past the beautiful bend,
Her memory lives on in those left behind,
Farewell my beloved, my soft-winged friend.
May a bright new horizon hold onto her dear,
And the touch of the breeze deem her soul near,
Her virtue shines bright as she's fading away,
Just is the teller, and never do fear.

When the last verse ended, she spoke. "This life is but a moment out of forever. I believe their souls will live on in paradise, where we will soon join them. A place where there will be no taste of pain, sorrow, or loss. It will all be celebration, glory, and peace."

Royal was still for a moment before stirring. "It is time." The three wordlessly stood to make their way to the landing grounds. The hive was dimly lit with small honeylamps, and other hymns like the one Nectar sang echoed through the halls. The hive held great respect for its oldest members who would leave today. Love and Pollen would also be missed by many who had sought their mentorship. At last, the three made it to the grounds where crowds of bees waited solemnly.

Standing upon the podium, Royal spoke. "Tonight is the night of our Parting Ceremony. We honor our eldest members who have chosen to leave the hive. Their decision blesses the hive greatly, yet their presence will be sorely missed. Tonight, we will have a word from anyone who departs. Tonight, we will bid them farewell, but not forever." She added, "As you know, two mentors leave the hive tonight.

I want to announce that a new mentor will be ready to help you tomorrow. His name is Courage." The crowd rippled in surprise, but didn't challenge it.

Royal stepped aside for the line of bees who would leave tonight. Orchid spoke first. "I have been honored to be a part of the liberation of this hive. I have seen us all at our worst, and now we are headed toward our best! I hope my departure will ensure that one more bee is properly nourished this Flowersleep. Thank you all, and Lighthive bless." She dipped her head and stepped down.

Several small speeches filled the evening. Many of them came from bees who had spent most of their lives under Lilac and Buzzz's reign. Many spoke of a ray of hope and promise for a peaceful future, and sentimental tears were shed. It was especially beautiful, since during the tyrannical reign, moments like this did not exist. Bees were ruthlessly killed or forcibly removed rather than being given a choice. Now, each departing member was seen and heard before willingly leaving. They were appreciated and honored accordingly.

After a while, Pollen and Love were the last to speak. Love went first. "Hive Honey Quest, each and every one of you is most dear to me. I have been honored to connect with so many more of you in the last few weeks. If you take anything from me, remember that you are cherished and valued. Know that the Light is with you, and that you can be free! Free to love one another as you are loved. I will miss you all, until we are reunited once again." Her eyes sparkled with tears.

Pollen was next. The clearing was dead silent as she hesitated to begin. "Friends. Sisters. Brothers. I, like many of us, have seen Lighthive's glory in this hive. We've been set free from tyrannical reign and have grown closer than I imagined possible. I am humbled that you have chosen me to lead in various ways. It has been my greatest pleasure." She took a shaky breath. "Be watchful, dear ones. Be aware of darkness that can grow in secret. The only way is the Light, which crushes every shadow in the blink of an eye. It will equip you with awareness and sight. It will be your armor and your strength. I pray that you will all feel the warmth of the sun and taste fresh nectar once again."

With that, Pollen stepped down, and the crowd erupted into tearful cheers. Royal gathered her friends into a long hug. "You'll be sorely missed, my girls. Find the sweetest bit of nectar left out there." She took a moment with each she-bee: Love, Trust, Faith, Peace, and Pollen.

There were a couple hundred bees leaving today. They all gathered at the hive's entrance after saying their goodbyes. Then, they began to fly out, singing another hymn together. It started out quiet and bittersweet before swelling into something almost joyful.

Evening shadows cross the plain,
Golden hour paints the trees,
Never you forget my name,
Feel my warmth within the breeze.
As my own day's end is near,
Feel the wind beneath my wings,
And before I disappear,
Hear the gentle song I sing.
Think of me with pleasantry,
Do not hate my passing by,
Once again your face i'll see,
In the plains of the most high.

Just like that, they were gone. The hive was completely silent. They sat in vigil until the sun slipped below the horizon outside. Royal was briefly left alone with her thoughts. The clearing was almost empty after most observers had retired to their rooms. With a jolt, she realized she shouldn't be alone - it was unsafe considering the dangers within the hive. She stood to briskly make her way to the throne room. But before she could go, someone grabbed her hand.

"Queen Royal!" Royal let out a sigh of relief when she saw it was just Nectar, her dear little nurse bee. "Oh, I'm sorry, I hope I didn't scare you!" Nectar immediately realized her mistake.

"No worries, friend. I'm glad you're with me. We should get to safety."

Nectar peered up at her Queen, her eyes troubled. "When and how will we handle the cult?"

"Soon. We must try to strike first. While logically it would be best if it happened before the doors close for Flowersleep any day now, I have a feeling that will not be the case. We need to wait for the right timing. Do you have any guidance on this?"

Nectar hesitated. "Lighthive has shared very little with me on this. I also agree that the right moment is important. We can't rush this, and we don't want to cause the hive intense confusion. I also believe that Courage will play a role in this, though I'm not sure how." She tilted her head. "What do you know about Courage?"

Royal shook her head. "I don't have enough time to know all my children deeply. But I do know that he fascinates me. He carries himself with maturity and wisdom unlike any other his age. I've always wondered about him ever since my difficult delivery. And now, Lighthive has chosen him to mentor the hive. He must be something special."

Nectar smiled. "You're right. While I'm not sure why, I know he's special too. I feel Lighthive's vibrations growing stronger whenever he speaks."

Royal blinked in wonder. "Well I have learned not to place undue pressure on any young bee. I have been too quick to place expectations on how life will happen, and Lighthive laughed. But I sure hope he is able to rise to his new role within the hive, and handle the pressure it will bring. I can see that in his position of importance, he may be key in helping guide the hive toward the Light."

The nurse bee nodded thoughtfully. "Only time will tell, I suppose."

Chapter 13: Informer

Hope was honestly terrified. The task before her was great, but she could do nothing else after her humbling misjudgement of New Beginning. She had to do this in order to make it up to the hive, and her mother, if it would be the last thing she'd do.

After her meeting with hive leadership, Queen Royal had pulled Hope aside for another word. "Thank you for coming clean with this information, Hope. But you must be very quick to resume the tasks they have given you for now."

"What?" Hope had buzzed in confusion. "They want me to recruit bees... and position the group to take over the hive."

Royal nodded with dark eyes. "I'm aware of this. Hope, you hold a powerful position within the group. Leaving now would already risk your life. But you can choose to stay, and provide an inside view of the group's plans as they develop. This would also risk your life, but you'd do so protecting the hive like a warrior." She hesitated. "Of course, this is your decision to make. If you choose to leave, I will have you protected with guards at all times."

Hope shook her head gravely. "No, you're right. This is how I can make things right. But mom... I can't report directly to you. If they discover my secret, they might follow me and find you vulnerable. I should speak through various messengers discreetly. I could make it appear as though I am trying to recruit them."

Royal's eyes glistened with proud tears as she looked down at her precious daughter. "I've missed you, Hope. And I am glad to have you back. You have great courage and resolve to serve the hive in this way. It turns out that even our mistakes can aid in our victories. No matter what, you have always been and will always be... loved."

Hope brought herself back to the present as a tear escaped her eye. She was filled with a new and powerful purpose. *I will make things right.* But she knew that NB might already be aware of her change. *They probably have eyes everywhere.* Hope took great care to appear as loyal as possible every moment of the day, even when she thought she was alone.

While Hope was a bit afraid, she felt lighter than ever after revealing the truth to her friends. It gave her a spark she had been missing for a while. She decided she'd let that spark fuel her starring role as "loyal servant" of New Beginning. *They will easily mistake it for passion and drive.* Today, she was supposed to begin the process of recruitment. She decided she would take time to observe the landing grounds and try to target possible recruits.

Hope knew she didn't want to drive more bees to join New Beginning, and she wasn't sure how to approach this. But somehow, maybe she could recruit others who could protect her secret. That way, she could start a small force of "traitors" within. But she knew she'd need to choose very carefully. *And I probably shouldn't choose close friends, because New Beginning is likely aware of all my connections.* She was suddenly struck by her own thoughts. Did they perhaps choose her for leadership because she was close to the Queen? She burned with anger at the thought. *They just wanted to use my position to their advantage!* Trying to conceal her fluctuating emotions, she rested at the edge of the landing grounds to watch the passerbees.

Bees were busy and fun to watch. Few lingered for more than a few minutes, but if they did, it was to rest or enjoy the sunlight streaming in from the hive entrance. Hope inspected several bees thoughtfully. *How does one identify their target?* She thought back to when she was approached by Goldie, and remembered the words Sun had said about securing new recruits. *They appeal to the ego. But I don't want to do that. I'm looking for something different.*

Not really knowing what she was looking for, she allowed her eyes to dance from bee to bee as she made assumptions about them based on their appearance, expression, or speed of gate. Some were in a focused hurry with no room for interruption. Others looked tired and battered from a chilly pollination run. Some bees had faces set with wisdom or self-assuredness, and others with a bright beginner's zeal. Some exuded confidence, while others looked either insecure or eager to prove themselves. *I suppose I need someone who is honest and wise, with a warrior's taste for goodness and justice.*

In the middle of that thought, her eyes landed on a familiar face. A sturdy drone with messy fur from a recent flight was grooming himself discreetly in the clearing, when he met her gaze. *Is he perhaps far enough removed from me to be safe? I truly don't know him all that well, but I know he is trustworthy. There are probably no known ties between us as we hardly were seen together. And he was not made famous in the war...*

"Hope?" She jolted as she realized the drone had approached her. His face bore a riddled expression and a cautious smile. "Goodness me, it's actually you!"

"Thistle! Long time no see, huh?" Hope was a little sheepish. While her interactions with the drone had been minimal, they had worked as quite an excellent team in battle, and would always share in the memories of war and victory. It seemed like Thistle hadn't missed a beat. He was as strong and alert as ever.

"Where have you been?" Thistle's cautious smile grew into a grin. He looked at her expectantly.

"Actually, it's a long story. Do you have time?"

Thistle glanced around him. "I could pull some strings..." He chuckled. "Just kidding, I'm free. Do you want to go for a flight?"

"Sure!" Hope felt a strange, small flutter in her belly. Usually drones might ask a bee on a flight as a sort of romantic gesture. But of course, this was not the case. They simply had a lot to discuss.

The two passed the hive guards unchallenged as they made their way toward the edge of the forest. It was many moments before anyone spoke, since speaking in flight often involved shouting. Instead, Thistle sped up, glancing back at her playfully. "Catch me if you can!"

He increased in speed, and Hope chased him. She pursued him through the strangest nooks of the forest. Near its floor, they flew through a bunched root from a giant oak tree that scooped out of the ground. They navigated through precarious thickets and riddled brush. Hope laughed freely as she allowed herself to have fun for the first time in a while. After maybe ten minutes of play, they reached the edge of the forest and Thistle gestured toward the ground.

As they approached the grass Hope let out an awestruck gasp. Between the thick blades, a lone flower stood proud in full bloom. It was a brilliant blue iris. It proudly tackled the overwhelming sea of shriveled grass around it and peaked out just enough to gather all of the sun's rays. "Wow!" She beamed. "This is the most beautiful flower I've... ever seen! And so late in the season!" She couldn't manage to say anything else while she took it in.

Thistle landed on the glorious flower to rest. He gestured at the mouth of the flower, inviting Hope to have a sip. Without thinking, she obliged. It was the best nectar any bee would find so close to Flowersleep. She reveled in the sweet taste, as if she were in her own world. After some time, she suddenly realized that she had left Thistle just basking in the sun as she feasted.

"Oh, forgive me, Thistle!" She laughed brightly. "You've just made my day, and I couldn't seem to resist! How did you find this gem when you yourself don't have the means to pollinate and collect nectar?"

Thistle smiled. "I like to spend some of my free time finding beauties like this. I don't often get the chance to show them to anyone." He looked at her warmly. "But when I saw you again, I knew I had to!"

Hope sat next to Thistle cautiously. "I know I've been distant from everyone I've known for quite some time. I can explain everything."

After a deep breath, Hope began telling the long story of what had happened. She left out no details, and felt at ease doing so since she was far from the surveilled hive. Thistle listened intently, a fire burning in his eyes. Hope took another sighing breath to conclude the lengthy tale.

"I knew our victory wouldn't mean instantaneous peace, but this?" Thistle fidgeted with his hands. "This is worse than I thought. I want to help somehow."

Hope sighed. "Your help would be useful. But you have to know that this is going to be dangerous. My goal is to bring in a couple of fellow informers." Her voice had dropped to a whisper out of habit. "You realize that you'd be risking your life."

Thistle looked at her with determination. "Hope, I am always looking for a way to serve the hive honorably. And I will continue to do so until the day I die."

Hope looked at him with admiration. "Thistle, as long as I've known of you, you have never missed an opportunity to help others. Don't you ever get scared? Don't you ever feel the pressure?"

He paused thoughtfully. "Yes, I do."

"Then how do you do it? How are you so abandoned?"

"I guess I just know that the lives of others - their happiness, safety, and freedom - mean more than my own desires. I will do anything to give others the life they deserve."

Hope blinked, lowering her gaze. "I wish you had some of that to share. I could use a generous dose."

"Well, if you hang out with me enough, it might just rub off on you." Thistle laughed warmly. Hope laughed right along with him. She detected something in his statement; he seemed to be affectionate toward her. She tilted her head at him oddly and studied his face. The two grew silent together as they studied each other's eyes.

Hope broke the silence. "Thistle, I haven't felt this joyful and free in a long time. Thank you."

Thistle smiled. "Anytime, really! Though the hive could sadly be sealed off any day."

"Well if you go through with helping me, I'll be seeing you every day within the hive." She buzzed. The two enjoyed some playful conversation for a while as the sun crossed the sky. It was close to sunset when Hope started. "Oh no, I have to be at a New Beginning meeting very soon! Do you want to come tonight, or start tomorrow?"

"I'll come." Thistle stood and they took off toward the hive. It was not a long flight, since they flew in a straight line this time. As the hive came into view, they noticed a strange blue sheet draping over the top and sides of their home. A few bees were swarming about in a panic. "Oh, what happened here?"

Chapter 14: Flowersleep Is Near

"The Honeybandits came again to make some Flowersleep preparations. They inspected the hive and removed excess debris. Then, they placed something over us, perhaps to keep us dry?" A hive guard was able to answer Hope's questions.

She glanced around, noticing that many bees had begun working at the hive entrance. They were creating bee glue to reduce the hive entrance size. Bee glue was just one of many substances expertly designed by bees. The entrance would become smaller and smaller until it was ready to be totally closed. It was clear that the cold was imminent in order to trigger this instinctual response.

Hope looked at the Thistle with sad eyes. "I knew this would be coming soon, but it's so much earlier than usual, from what I've heard. Who knows how long we'll be trapped within." She quietly but swiftly strode through the landing grounds, gesturing for Thistle to follow. They had no more time to spare. She began to lead him toward the dark corner where New Beginning held meetings. Suddenly, Pea cried out.

"Hope! And Thistle, hello!" She chased after her friend. "How are you doing?" Pea looked back and forth between the two, her eyes expressing uncertainty.

Hope nodded affirmingly. "He knows." Looking at her friend, she added, "Sweet Pea... It's always good to see you, my friend. Unfortunately I have to be off if I'm to... maintain my standing with NB."

Pea paused. "Hope, would it be impossible for me to help? Would it blow your cover?"

"I'm not sure." Hope smiled cautiously. "It's definitely a risk, Pea. And I don't want you to get hurt. If I had my way, you'd be safe on the opposite side of the hive, tucked away."

"Hope, I really want to help. I don't want to lose you again." Pea stared meaningfully at her friend. "If my presence won't disrupt the plan, then I'd rather risk myself to help our cause than to hide away in safety." The she-bee shook her wings and stood tall.

Hope closed her eyes and took a breath. "I believe we should be safe enough for now. I'd be happy for your help." She smiled, a tear escaping her eye. She resisted from giving her friend a warm hug, in case New Beginning was watching. "But we need to hurry!"

The three hustled to get to the meeting as soon as they could. They arrived just a few minutes late, and settled quietly at the back of the crowd. Hope looked around in bewilderment. *The gathering is noticeably larger today.* She settled in between her two friends as Goldie spoke.

"Welcome new and old members! You have found yourselves a community of bees who you can call family!" She paused as the crowd cheered. "Tonight is a social event. There will be dancing and feasting. Always remember that happiness can be found here, with all of your friends. May the festivities begin!"

"It's almost as if they have no clue that the hive entrance is sealing up as we speak!" Hope murmured to Thistle and Pea. "Listen, I have to be here for the entirety of this, as well as afterward for a leadership meeting. I'm... terrified. But for now, we have to blend in." She backed away to find space, and began to mirror a beedance from a member nearby. She executed each move perfectly, since dancing had been a common pastime in New Beginning. She glanced up at her friends encouragingly, and found Thistle gazing at her with admiration. She laughed nervously. "Pea, your turn!"

Sweet Pea replicated the dance pretty well, but struggled with some of the unusual moves. She smiled. "I can almost forget my troubles." She winked at Hope.

Hope could not deny the pit in her stomach. The gathering dragged on, and yet it was going by so fast somehow. Her dread kept growing as time passed. She knew that soon, she'd have to meet with the leadership of New Beginning. Not knowing how much they were or weren't aware of, she could very well be walking right into her execution. *I need to be strong.* Hope tried to relax as she danced with her friends. In between songs, she eyed the snack table woefully. It was lined with small late-season flowers and bowls of honey. *What a time to be feasting. Right at the very brink of Flowersleep hunger.* Hope tried to hide her disgust.

The music slowed down for a song or two, and Hope's thoughts were interrupted by a tap on her shoulder. "Care to dance with me, Hope?" She turned around, expecting to see Thistle. But it wasn't him. It was Theo. Hope froze, and tried to hide her high-strung nerves.

"Of course, Theo." She looked around for a moment to try and spot her friends, but they were swallowed into the crowd.

"Looking for someone?" Theo buzzed.

"Ah, yes, just a couple of my recent recruits. I want to make sure they are having the best time possible."

Theo smirked. "They will!" He pulled her onto the floor and the two began swaying, a bit awkwardly. After a few moments of silence, Theo spoke again. "Hope, how on earth did you secure leadership here?" His eyes glistened with wistfulness. "I've been trying to work my way up for months." He seemed to have recovered from his anger for the most part, but his curiosity was quite sharp and fiery.

Hope cleared her throat. "Um, well I didn't do anything, really! I think they chose me due to my family connections." She added, "They must think I can recruit some important members."

Theo tilted his head with interest. "Well either way, you know you won't be going hungry this Flowersleep!" He twirled her. "What are they like?"

Hope looked confused. "Who?"

"The council, of course. The overseers of the group."

"Oh, well they are... powerful, smart, and... different than I had expected." She was struggling with this conversation. At what seemed like the perfect moment, the two were interrupted.

"Theo!" Thistle exclaimed. The two drones were face-to-face again for the first time in a while. Hope winced. She could see a trace of hurt veiled behind Thistle's optimistic expression, but he hid it well.

"Thistle..." Theo grunted awkwardly. "You're new here."

"Yes! Isn't it great? Why haven't you told me about it sooner?" Thistle asked his brother enthusiastically. "I haven't really seen you." As the brothers attempted to converse, Hope noticed the music had died, and the crowd was beginning to file out with lighthearted banter. She glanced at Thistle apologetically and waved before slipping away. The gathering was coming to an end, and she was expected to join the leaders shortly. As she navigated through the crowd, she was also able to wave goodbye to Sweet Pea, showing gratitude in her expression.

As Hope approached the back meeting room, the earth was frozen. The air seemed thick, and her heart raced. Her brain was paralyzed, void of any thought but what was ahead of her. When she reached the door, it took every ounce of her self-control to turn the handle instead of flying away. *This time, I'm not going to run away from what I fear. This time, I'm going to do the right thing.* Taking a breath, she entered the room.

She was horrified to discover that she was the last of the leaders to make it there. All eyes were on her as she took her seat. Sun sat at the head of the table like usual. Today, Goldie was at her side taking meeting notes. This wasn't unusual, though she didn't attend every meeting.

Sun sat erect, facing the newest leaders with intensity. She began to speak. "I would like to hear about your recent successes, newcomers. What did you accomplish?"

The other new she-bee piped up, her voice proud. "I have recruited seventeen new bees. I believe I've selected prime new members. They are young, zealous, and loyal. In addition to that, I have overseen some late-season contributions to our personal honey stores."

The drone also responded. "I protected our stores during the Honeybandit's antics, and oversaw the repair and replenishing of any damaged comb. I also worked with some promising young drones in the group who will prove helpful when a battle arises. I plan to start building interest in combat, and training them."

Sun turned to Hope expectantly. Hope's heart raced. *I haven't done anything compared to the others... What can I say?* She straightened in her seat and cleared her throat. "I... well, I have only recruited two new members today." A few of the leaders with greater seniority stared with disappointment. Hope continued. "...My focus has been elsewhere recently. I have been making my way back into the good graces of hive leadership." She wasn't sure if this would be a good thing to say, but she saw no other option. "I'm working on winning their trust and comradery again. I believe that it may be very useful when we choose to make our move."

The room grew silent. Goldie scribbled words onto her birch paper frantically. Sun's expression grew from skeptical to overwhelmingly satisfied. "Excellent idea, Hope!" She paused. "I heard word that you've been interacting with some important members of the hive, and I wasn't sure what was going on there. I now know that I was wrong to worry. Because of your connection with the Queen, we may secure victory much more easily. When the time comes, you will be the perfect assassin."

Chapter 15: Season's End

Courage thought carefully before responding. "Yes, that is true. Hardship is inevitable. But hardship isn't to only be seen as negative. If all was perfect and dandy, we might become complacent in our comfort. Lighthive uses the struggles we endure for our greater good. They help us develop good character and strong faith. So, we are not to hate - or even just tolerate - difficult times, but we are to take joy in them."

"Take joy?" The drone laughed, anguished. "That's rich. Am I supposed to take joy in the fact that my closest family was lost in the war?"

Courage's face grew compassionate. "I'm sorry for your loss, Aspen." He remained quiet for a long time, as the drone began to fall apart. He began to cry into his hands as the pressure of his undealt with emotions overpowered him. Courage placed a comforting hand on his thorax as he wept. He did not speak a word. He was just there. After several minutes, Aspen tried to speak, but his voice cracked as more tears fell.

"There is comfort in the Light... and always a safe place to feel and to grieve. It may never feel right that they are gone, especially at the hands of evil. But one day, all will be known, and our hearts will be healed. There will never be another sorrow, and all will be right."

Aspen slumped forward as he soaked in Courage's words. After a long while, he straightened in his chair. "Thank you, Courage. It felt good to let that out. I have a lot to think about."

Courage smiled sympathetically, accepting a brief hug from the drone before he left. "See you in a week or two?" He called after him. Aspen nodded as he left.

Courage was left with his thoughts, and his heavy heart. Aspen was his last student of the day, and it sure had been a long one. After Pollen and Love left for the Parting Ceremony, they left a void behind, and everyone missed them. Courage became one of only two approved mentors within the hive, and he had been working non-stop. Nectar had many other duties, so she only mentored part-time. He felt the weariness in his bones and soul. *If it weren't for Lighthive, I would have reached my end by now.*

Courage had been learning a lot as he met so many hurting bees. Their stories, struggles, and questions were of every sort. Courage never knew exactly what he would say. He had nothing written down to refer to for tough questions. Instead, words flowed from him like an endless river. There was a lot that felt familiar. *I suppose those are things I knew in my past.* He didn't strive for answers, and so he was not tired for that reason. It was more of a weariness he felt, like how rocks bend and groan as water powerfully carves through the landscape. Courage felt he was being changed, and while it wasn't without its discomforts, he began to feel more and more like himself. *My true self.*

Gathering his things, he left his appointment room with a tired sigh and began the walk to his cell. He took into account the results of the Honeybandit's work. Some bees had begun to repair and tidy the hive, while others slowly tended to the hive entrance. *When the frost comes, the door will be sealed for many long months. Then, we may be facing a dark and scary foe.* He blinked in confusion at his own thoughts. *A dark and scary foe?* But Courage's mind was tired of making connections, so he filed it away. As he reached his cell, he fell right into his cushion, thinking of Meadow longingly as he drifted to sleep.

ROYAL LOOKED OUT UPON the scene before her. The sun was barely climbing over the horizon, and a cold gust of wind battered her face. Squinting, she saw exactly what she had expected to see. Nectar stood beside her.

"The frost has come, my Queen."

Royal nodded. "Just like you had said." She hesitated, her voice laced with fear. "It is so much earlier than usual. And while I expected that to be the case, it doesn't bode well for the situation with NB. Just how am I to handle that when the hive is sealed?"

Nectar spoke softly. "There's always the chute."

Royal nodded slowly. All hives had to leave a small chute open to keep the hive clean throughout Flowersleep. They would chuck debris, waste, or dead bees out that way. "That may be the best course of action. However, the chute is often quite narrow. It would be impossible to use at a large scale if that became necessary." She hesitated. "Would it be unwise to make the chute wider this year?"

"It would not be advisable. Everybee works very hard to keep you and themselves warm in the cold season. Extra drafts could be risky." Nectar smiled. "If it helps, I feel the peace of Lightive about this."

Royal took a long breath. "Thanks Nectar. My nerves have been high strung recently, and I haven't even had the chance to properly grieve. Our dear friends... the hive feels empty without them." She was silent for a moment before she continued. "How is Courage doing as a mentor? It's quite a heavy load for such a young bee, and he carries the brunt of the mentorship load currently. Has Lighthive revealed any additional appointees?"

Nectar shook her head. "I haven't had any new guidance on that. Let me know if you do! As for Courage, he seems to be handling this quite well. He is steadfast, and exudes peace." Nectar's eyes twinkled curiously. "I keep on grasping for anything about him from Lighthive, but they are being miserly."

The two chuckled. Royal turned to her little nurse bee, as her expression changed. She was vulnerable, and her eyes misted. "Nectar, I can't imagine leading the hive without you. Please, don't age."

Nectar smiled sadly. "I am beginning to feel some of the tells of age, but I do think I will be around longer yet. Soon, I will take up a special apprentice and teach her all the ways of a nurse bee. But I can't choose until the right bee presents herself." The small worker hugged Royal for a long time. "I'm not going anywhere yet." She consoled her.

As the morning sun rose higher, the hive began to stir. Royal assembled herself and the small collection of early risers in the landing grounds, and waited as the crowd swelled. Sting also joined her side to support her, as he always did. After quite some time, she began her announcement. "Hive Honey Quest and all those within, good morning! Today, I regret to inform you that the frost has come. The hive will be completely sealed by the end of today. I will be personally assembling teams, and Nectar will oversee them. Those who aren't busy can enjoy one more day in nature, as the warmth of the sun relieves the earth. Go soak in the sun. But take care to be back by sunset tonight so that you won't be trapped outside. Please, enjoy today."

The crowd disbanded as bees buzzed and murmured amongst themselves. Nectar began arranging teams to work at the hive entrance, and made arrangements for the chute as well. Meanwhile, Royal stood next to her King, just watching the bees of her hive. It warmed her heart to see them as they took off in excitement for a final flight of the season. However, it was bittersweet. Royal knew that Flowersleep would challenge them greatly. Food rationing would need to take place if they wanted to make it, especially after all the honey that was taken from them this year. *The Honeybandits have too much faith in us.*

Sting touched her hand comfortingly. "My love, your heart is heavy and your mind is burdened."

Royal melted under her King's affections. She turned toward him and sighed. "Yes, my love. You're right."

"I want to let you know that training has been going well."

Royal had given Sting a big job in preparation for the clash with NB. He was training some of the hive drones, especially ones who had seen battle before. Thistle was one of them, among others.

"Every morning, they practice battle techniques in close quarters. I started it "for fun", and the drones were happy to join in. No one suspects anything at this time."

"That's great, Sting. Thank you."

Sting touched her face. "Today, I have worked with Nectar to arrange some rest for you. So, come with me to your throne room. I'm going to give you some relaxing treatments and woo you with my incredible charm." He smiled playfully.

Royal couldn't help but cry. She looked at Sting with deep admiration and love. "You have no idea how much that means to me. It might be hard to rest my mind, but I will try." She followed him toward her throne room, already feeling a bit lighter.

Chapter 16: Crescendo

It would be a bittersweet day like it was every year. This year, it came early. The delicate silver frost had melted quickly at the sun's mercy, but it threatened to return again with a vengeance at night. Bees never really saw Flowersleep. Frost was enchanting, mysterious, and intimidating. While some forest creatures might spend the season in hibernation though, the bees would spend it awake and alert in their sealed hive.

Their heavily worked bodies would rest and recuperate after many long months of making honey and other miraculous solutions. They would face the threat of cold, disease, and starvation. The Queen would lay little to no eggs during this time, which would shift her entire focus in the hive. It was always a challenging mental and emotional shift to make, but her body would appreciate the rest. And everyone would have to learn to coexist and adapt until the cold was gone and Flowerbud was upon them.

Hive Honey Quest's members were scattered today, grasping onto the last threads of the life they loved. Hope and Thistle had slipped away for one more jaunt in nature together. Sweet Pea had set out on a final adventure to some of her favorite familiar places outside as well. Royal did her best to take her mind off of things and enjoyed her King's thoughtful gestures. She took a deep breath and let it all go for just a moment. Nectar supervised the work at the entrance of the hive until the sun dipped low, and more stragglers made their way home.

The nursery comb was being tended to by the doctor bees and caretakers as some of the last new arrivals emerged from their cells. Builder bees scoured the hive to make sure every drafty crevice was properly sealed for their warmth and protection. Maid bees cleared debris from the hive and the planners arranged living situations for each hive member over Flowersleep. Scientists, flower specialists, and other more outside-based workers gathered what they could before the hive was sealed. Fighters enjoyed a few final matches as well, hovering just outside the hive.

The day had passed by with merciless speed. As the sky turned into beautiful bright colors, the cold chill made its presence known. Many bees slipped out to briefly enjoy the sunset once more, returning quickly to the warmth of the hive. After waiting for as long as they could, the announcement was made, and the hive was sealed for the season. Everyone was silent, knowing full well that the road ahead wasn't easy. Most retired to their own spaces for the night to brood.

Joy lay in the middle of the empty landing grounds, staring at the black abyss of darkness above her. *I hope I will be able to taste fresh nectar again.* She closed her eyes, visualizing the lush meadows in the peak of summer, brimming with every variety of wildflower. She had remembered from the earlier announcement that food would be rationed daily over Flowersleep so that they'd have the best chances of pulling through. It was going to be different.

Joy was ripped from her thoughts as she suddenly noticed a presence beside her. She sat up and opened her eyes, a bit alarmed. It was just Courage. Smiling, she relaxed back down onto the floor next to her brother. "It's you!"

Courage laughed. "I'm so sorry, my hope was to not disturb you, sister!" The young drone peered thoughtfully toward the high ceiling. "I had today off. It was very restful. What did you do today?"

A sting of regret pierced Joy's heart. "Oh, I had assumed you would be busy! I wish I had spent today with you!" Her eye produced a vigorous tear. She rarely got to connect with her brother, who was so needed in the hive. She missed him all the time, but had accepted the new reality and adapted. She had learned to live her life more solo. But knowing she had missed an opportunity to be with him was terrible indeed.

"I'm here now, sister! And it was as much on my end as yours."

"What did you do today?" Joy asked, still sore about it.

Courage looked toward her. "No one had a session today with the hive sealing, so I took one last trip to the Honeycrystal."

Joy's eyes grew wide. "In this weather?" A trip to the Honeycrystal was precarious enough without cold, powerful winds. She looked at him in wonder. "Courage, you are truly something else. Why did you go?"

Courage shifted. "I just felt... disconnected. I wanted to see someone."

Joy's eyes narrowed. "Are you sure you went to the Honeycrystal? Or were you visiting your special friend?" She bumped his shoulder playfully. "Meadow?"

"Well, I did see Meadow too, once more."

Joy's excitement faded for a moment. "Brother, how will you fare not getting to see her during all of Flowersleep? In fact, part of me thought that maybe today, you'd run off to be with her. But you're still here. That has to be hard."

Courage hesitated for a long time. "Joy, there is so much I wish I could tell you. But for now, be at peace knowing that I'll be alright. I'm here in Hive Honey Quest for a reason - I can feel it. I can't go now. I can't run from my destiny."

"How do you know what your destiny is?" Joy paused. "I am still so uncertain of mine. Most days, I just feel like another bee in a sea of bees."

"No matter how grandiose or ordinary your role is, it is important." Courage offered. "It takes a lot of really good bees to run a good hive."

"I suppose I'm happy to be an ordinary bee." Joy smiled, reconsidering. "It can be a little lackluster, but all I have to do each day is my best. In your case, you are expected to perform perfectly, and to help others all day long! I don't know how you do it!"

"I feel like every bee is ordinary, but each is given their own tasks. You can do those well, or you can slack off. But if you do well with whatever position you hold, you will feel more fulfilled, and will bless whoever is around you. There is no harm in having a quiet, consistent, hard-working, and humble life. I think it's absolutely beautiful."

Joy smiled for a moment while she soaked in those words. Then she shook her head and said, "Silly me, I'm sure you've had enough supporting others for the week. How are you?" She asked the question, looking into her brother's eyes.

Courage looked back reassuringly. "I am... well. I am doing so well. My heart is full. That's honestly all I can say." He sat still, his expression purely content. "Tell me sister, how did you end up spending the day?"

Joy sighed dreamily. "I mostly just sunbathed, and said goodbye to my favorite trees and landmarks. Just in case I never see them again."

"I am certain you will." Courage smiled.

The day inevitably came to an end, and the two farewelled and parted to go to their cells. Soon, all in the hive were asleep.

AHEAD, HIVE HONEY QUEST would face many trials and difficulties. The new, regimented lifestyle that came with the cold was hard to adapt to after the freedom of Flowerripe. For a few weeks, some bees were stealing more honey than they were rationed. It went unnoticed for some time, but soon it became apparent that they weren't on schedule. Hive planners and leadership quarreled to get things under control.

Tensions ran high in the hive. Some dealt with depression as the lifestyle shift took its toll. Bees who had worked mostly outside were more greatly affected. Courage was still the only full-time mentor, and his schedule was completely swamped to keep up with the demand.

New Beginning had ceased growing, and focused more within the group. Changes were made quickly as Sun and other leaders moved toward their goals. Hope continued to work inside, and was still undiscovered. She reported whenever possible to various messengers, and both Pea and Thistle continued supporting her inside NB. The three tried to identify any bees who may be doubting, to see if they could free them from the brainwashing. Progress was slow though, and things were getting bad within the group.

Royal, Sting, and Nectar worked on a plan to handle New Beginning. Nectar repeatedly stated that timing was important, and it wasn't now. Meanwhile, Courage still learned more and more from Lighthive, and guided the hive members as best as he could. There were many bees who grew in faith through the hardship, and while times were dark and challenging, there was a silver lining of hope amidst it all. The hive lay in wait.

Chapter 17: The Imposter

"Our time is nearing, New Beginning!" Sun stood before the large crowd with triumph. She was wearing a vibrant monarch wing as a cape, like usual, and the crowd buzzed with excitement to see their elusive leader. The hive had been sealed for about 2 months now, and things had really been changing.

Hope stood next to Pea and Thistle in the crowd. She tried not to look obviously brooding, but she was deeply troubled. New Beginning changed so quickly over the last couple months, ever since the hive was sealed and the group stopped accepting new recruits. It was clear they had refocused on the minds of the members. In a short time, she watched bright young bees fade into obedient members who believed the group was superior to any other in the hive. That became increasingly obvious to Hope ever since she had quietly retracted her own loyalty to NB.

Somehow, each member now believed that the current hive leadership was insufficient. They all became hopelessly loyal and committed to New Beginning and whatever Sun wanted. They were sold out, especially after Sun exposed her Thelytoky nature a month ago. They trusted her blindly, and believed she would be the best Queen. If they had questions or concerns, they were never voiced.

Over time, bees began slowly relocating to stay in the New Beginning corner of the hive all the time. While they thought they did it willingly, it was actually required. Hope knew this because in the leadership meetings, Sun had outlined that this would be necessary to move into phase two. And Sun didn't exactly leave room for disobedience. Before long, every member lived together, sharing their warmth. Their interests were to support the group, not the hive.

Leaving the group was reserved for group business, like honey raids. Hope specifically got to leave often to "continue a normal relationship with Royal, for leverage", but Pea and Thistle could hardly get away. She felt sorry for them, but had little energy left to help cheer them up. Hope had been in a tough and meticulous position, fearing each day that she'd be discovered. She faced having to share information about Royal and other hive leadership. Sometimes, she was able to conceal the truth, but other times, she had to share things to maintain her validity in this role. Ultimately, she did what she needed to do so that she could help protect her loved ones.

Meetings in NB had mostly shifted from fun, interactive dances and feasts to more formal lectures. The group felt less like a community these days, and more like an army. Everybee had to follow orders blindly, and individuals lost their sovereignty and spark. According to Hope, it seemed like Sun planned to shed light on the group's ultimate plan this very day.

She continued speaking in her proud and authoritative tone. "New Beginning is the future of this hive. Queen Royal and other hive leadership have let everyone down! With food stores running lower than ever and disease plaguing some parts of the hive, she simply cannot remain in power. Instead, we will take control. We will liberate the hive from her failure! We will take what should rightfully be ours!"

The crowd erupted into passionate cheers. Hope stood silent, clapping to show mock support. She glanced sideways at her friends. Pea struggled to conceal the devastation in her eyes. Hope knew with certainty that she would have to talk with Royal as soon as possible.

"In a week, we will begin. Before then, raid as much of the remaining honey stores in the hive as you can. We must be strong and well fed for this endeavor! My leaders will guide you in what other steps need to be taken as we prepare."

As Sun descended the stairs, she silently gestured for her leaders to follow. Hope glanced at Thistle and Pea worriedly before slipping away to join the meeting. *It's happening.*

Sun sat at the head of the table with confidence. "Our time is here. I have very important jobs for you all." She looked at her leaders, beginning to explain various details of her intricate plan. Hope took mental notes of anything helpful. "I need you to prioritize the battle training this week. Every drone should be ample, as well as all the workers who have the zeal. Any other worker should be focused on raids. We need to siphon honey fast as well to make a bigger dent. We will add that honey to our current private stores."

Sun turned to Hope. "Your role is critical in this. You will be getting hive leadership into a vulnerable position for us. We need to eliminate Royal quickly and smoothly if we wish to be successful. Only then will the hive be sufficiently confused and disarmed."

Hope tamed her repulsion within. "What's the plan?"

"We need to lead Royal, Sting, and Nectar into the center of the landing grounds. They must be as unaccompanied as possible, and there will be no time to dawdle. When they are where we want them to be, jump away to safety. They will be destroyed by a murder ball. Other members will keep hive bees at bay as the task is completed."

"I need to set this up correctly with leadership. I have an idea for how to get them all there together." Hope spoke. "When can I meet with them to put this story into motion?"

Sun buzzed firmly. "You are very needed right now; I think that connecting with them the day before we strike will be sufficient. Until then, you will focus your purpose and energy into our preparations."

Hope had a sinking feeling. *I won't even be able to speak to them until the day before?* "I want to offer that hive leadership may be very curious as to my whereabouts. Lately, I've connected with them frequently. They may even come looking for me if I don't meet them sooner."

Sun was unmoved. "It has already been decided, as well as the story. We believe that suspense will be helpful for the plan we've already formulated. Here's what we are going to do."

COURAGE YAWNED, EXHAUSTED from the day. Flowersleep was a difficult time for many bees, and since he was the only full-time hive mentor at this time, he was very busy. It amazed him how much he was learning, and he was honored by how much the hive members trusted him with their deepest struggles. Courage seemed to have a way about meeting everyone exactly where they were. He made them feel safe and heard.

As time went on, Courage had recognized countless shards of wisdom he had lost in the transition. Bees began to comment often that he was an old soul, and maturing very quickly. It was as if his past wisdom was being awakened within him, and he was therefore enabled to help others even better. He felt more and more like his true self.

Courage laid flat on his cushion, completely still, letting his exhaustion wash over him. It had been months since he had stopped meeting with Meadow. He was able to operate with a clearer mind because of that choice, but lately his longing to reconnect with her was increasingly distracting. *Meadow, I want to see you. Please...* He thought that just maybe, seeing his love would give him the boost he needed to keep working this hard. With a few deep breaths, he allowed himself to drift away into dreamland.

Meadow's eyes were the first thing he saw as he stirred. "My love." She buzzed, as smooth as honey.

Courage sat up, burying his face into her furry pelt and wrapping her in his arms. She buzzed contentedly before helping him up from the ground. He sighed. "I've missed you dearly." His gaze enveloped her, deep longing and desire showing through.

She smiled. "Every moment without you feels like a part of me is far away." After a moment, her face shifted into one of determination. "Listen, River. One of the key moments that triggered your journey back to earth is upon you. It arises as we speak."

Courage regrettably withdrew from his affection to focus. "I know... I can feel it now. It's something both tangible and untouchable at the same time..."

Meadow tilted her head. "Your intuition has sharpened. Do you know how to help?"

Courage pursed his lips thoughtfully. "I'm a hive mentor, but I am not usually welcome at hive leadership meetings. I'm not in the loop. But I think I should talk to Queen Royal to see what I can learn. She seems to regard me highly, so maybe she'll find it advantageous to share."

"That's a great first step. I hope you've also gotten quite comfortable with your combat training. While the inner war is far more dangerous, there's still a possibility that things could become physically threatening." Meadow shivered, trying to minimize her worry. "I don't want you to be in pain."

Courage smiled. "I'm ready to face whatever comes my way," Pausing, he added, "but what puzzles me more is how I can address the internal things. I mentor bees in the hive, but the ones who come to me are the ones who are seeking. They want guidance and support. Meanwhile, I can feel that the spirit that's growing within the corners of the hive is not as receptive. It's troubling, but almost unnoticeable. If I ignore it, it goes away completely. But the more I pay attention, the more it grows."

"What does the spirit feel like, River?"

"It feels like... well at first, it seemed harmless, even bright. Good. But as I kept tabs on it, it continued to grow. It now feels like a very dark, looming danger. But as I mentioned, If I wanted to, I could easily convince myself that it's still good." Courage shook his head, his hand on his forehead.

"Does it ring any bells, River?" Meadow peered at him expectantly. When he didn't have an answer, she buzzed with conviction. "The Imposter, River."

The name struck Courage. He knew right away that it wasn't good, but he couldn't remember why. "Talk to me."

"We dwell where the Light remains. The Light is truth and love. And you know of Darkhive, which tries to take the hearts of many. The Darkness blatantly spreads evil, hate, and so on. Now The Imposter... it presents as something very good. It preys on good, open bees and uses deception to win their hearts. Then, it makes them feel justified to do whatever they think they need to do, no matter the cost. But River, you must remember, The Imposter is a tool of Darkhive. It's simply a disguise."

It was all coming back to Courage now. The unease he'd had about the spirit was fully realized. "How, Meadow? How do I combat such an effective and powerful spirit?"

She touched his face. "You will not. The Light will. And you will be one of its vessels."

Chapter 18: Darkness

Royal's antennae ached. Hope hadn't been in communication with her for some time. Again, she hadn't been at the meeting today, and the Queen's concerns were great. *Has something happened to her? Or worse even...* Royal hated to consider it a possibility, but her relationship with Hope had been a swinging pendulum. A small part of her knew it was possible that Hope was not being truthful. Grunting, she cut off the thought. *I need to trust her.*

Royal was restless at her throne, surrounded by a small group of bees who were keeping the temperature of her room adequate. It was the dead of winter, and the cold that infiltrated the hive was threatening. Not only that, but the honey supply was running dangerously low. Most years, Flowersleep would persist for a few months before it was occasionally safe to venture out. By now, they would still have plenty of honey to last another month. But the cold had swept in a little early this year. The hive hadn't been prepared for an extra month of frost, and Royal wasn't sure if they would survive this. On top of that, honey stores were disappearing faster than usual, and she believed that NB was to blame.

Nectar sat beside her calmly. "You're brooding again, Your Highness."

"Yes, I suppose I am. The duties of a Queen are often too much to bear." Royal thought warmly of the King, who was currently busy elsewhere. "But the Light gives me strength. And let me tell you, yours and Sting's constant support is nothing short of a miracle to me every day."

The little nurse bee smiled, the lines deepening in her face. "I treasure our friendship." She turned her face to the Queen. "Share your thoughts with me, Royal. I can share the load."

Royal took a long sigh before quietly spilling her thought process. After a few minutes, she already began to feel a little bit lighter. Nectar was someone she could tell everything to. She didn't jump to conclusions or judge her ramblings and perceptions. Instead, she listened. She supported, and occasionally gave suggestions. But most importantly, she always brought it back to what mattered the most.

Royal took a long pause as she concluded, and Nectar's eyes were full of emotions. The nurse bee touched Royal's arm. "If it helps, I feel a great deal of peace. Somehow, Lighthive is going to pull us through this. I keep feeling within my abdomen that all will be well." She was lucid. "All of this - even the inner uprising - it *will* serve a purpose. After the War of the Ghost, we had a great gap to bridge. We were so lost, with no mutual basis." Nectar's wings trembled. "Evil is not born from the Light, but the Light makes it work together for our good in the long run. Trust me, all will be well."

The Queen soaked in those words, her eyes sparkling with tears. She crumbled and allowed peace to wash over her. Her fists relaxed, and she laid her hands open on her throne, turning her gaze upward. "So be it. Whatever we may face, it is in your hands." For a few moments, the two didn't say another word.

Five minutes had passed in silence when one of Royal's helpers entered the room. "Your Highness, Courage wishes to speak with you."

"Bring him in." She nodded, her curiosity piqued. She, of course, had always been fascinated by the drone, and hadn't been able to see him much since his appointment as a mentor. But in her mind, she regarded him as a part of the hive's leadership now. His wisdom had grown deep and steady and his work in the hive was integral to their survival during these trying times. In no time at all Courage entered the room, the door shutting quickly behind him to preserve the warmth within.

"Wow, it's so warm in here!" The drone had filled out a bit since she'd last seen him, and he was now presenting as a true adult. A soldier, even. He looked strong, determined, and confident.

"My son." Royal smiled to greet him. "What brings you to my throne room?"

Courage hesitated, seemingly unsure of how to proceed. He glanced toward Nectar, and then back at Royal.

"You don't need to worry. Anything you need to share with me is also safe with Nectar. She usually finds out anyway." Royal chuckled, her heart light at the sight of her son.

Courage took a breath, gathering himself. "Mother, I come asking for intelligence regarding what grows secretly within the hive. I have to help."

HOPE STIRRED. HER HEAD throbbed with sharp pangs. Confused, she blinked open her eyes. *Ouch!* Everything was blurry, dark, and cold. *Where am I? What happened?* She heaved herself halfway off the floor, rubbing her eyes gingerly. As her vision started to clear, she gasped. She was covered in bruises, on the floor of a dark prison. There seemed to be no entrance or exit to be found in the small room. She could see her own breath. Panicked, she grasped for any memories that could help explain her predicament. She sat motionless for several minutes.

All at once, it came back to her.

She had been discovered.

It was the day before the planned attack. Hope had joined the meeting with NB's leadership, and they were discussing how Hope would draw her mother into a position of danger. She had stayed undercover during the meeting, but afterward, she was suddenly confronted by the leaders. Apparently, the other worker who was recruited with her had become suspicious. She had been spying on her and happened to overhear a quiet, condemning conversation with Pea and Thistle. *Pea and Thistle!*

She whipped her head around, scanning for her friends. They were nowhere to be found. Her stomach was in knots as tears poured down her cheeks. *My friends...* She lowered herself to the floor, curling into a ball to cry. *My mother... Everyone I love is in danger. And I can't do anything about it.* She crumbled. She didn't move for at least an hour, her emotions completely overwhelming.

As her tears slowed, she twitched. Sluggishly, she pushed herself upright again. She knew that somehow, she had to push through and be strong. *I have to at least make sure there's absolutely no way out before I give up.*

Her muscles groaned in pain as she tried to stand. Everything hurt. Sighing, she paced toward one cold wall, touching it gingerly to look for any imperfections. She continued doing the same with every square inch. She got on her hands and knees to inspect the floor, trying to ignore her seizing joints, and then tried her best to test the ceiling. Despite her efforts, not a crack was found. It almost seemed as if there was no way in or out of the room she was trapped in. The bitter cold made it impossible for her to keep trying.

Hesitantly, she lowered herself to the floor in the center of the impenetrable cube, her head spinning. *Is this really how it ends?* She closed her eyes, tempted to submit to her exhaustion. She felt she was about to pass out as the warmth in her limbs was slowly ebbing away. Her mind slowed. Instead of frantic thoughts of survival, memories began to fill her vision. She saw her first flight outside, and the glory of the sunlight and plant life unfolding before her newborn eyes. She saw her first encounter with Lightwing, in all her brilliance. She reveled in bliss from within as she saw Thistle, staring into her eyes on that beautiful blue iris, and that powerful warmth enveloped her as she fell asleep.

Chapter 19: Murder Ball

Royal and Courage paced out of the throne room together. The Queen wore a determined expression as she strode toward the honey stores. The drone kept up, his face troubled. Shortly behind the two, Sting and Nectar followed. Before too long, the group of four made it to the honeycomb, their eyes wide. As it had been reported, a great deal of their remaining reserves had been plundered somehow even as they were being guarded. The honey they had counted on to make it through to Flowerbud was inevitably gone.

"It's impossible that NB actually ate all of that honey. They had to have stored it somewhere else in the hive." Courage offered, hopeful. It was likely true, but it didn't seem to mend the despair. For a moment, you could see a gleam of defeat in Royal's eyes. She was losing heart. *Is it time to intervene yet?* She pleaded within. *What should I do?*

As the hive leadership stood together, deciding how to proceed, Nectar straightened. "Your Majesty, we aren't alone here." There was no time to respond. The small nurse bee's eyes darted as fast as lightning to her side before hurling herself at the Queen with a shriek. *Oof!*

Just as Nectar had knocked the Queen away, Courage and Sting saw a projectile fly past where her head would have been. It was a rose thorn shard. With a sharp thud, the thorn embedded itself into the wooden wall of the hive. Sting cried out. "Stay down!" He and the four bees shifted to take shelter behind the frame in the opposite direction of their attacker. "Don't move!"

The group huddled together as two more thorns skimmed their antennae. One sliced Courage's left antennae, and he suppressed a yelp. Peering into the hive's shadows, Royal watched as figures began to emerge with speed. Seeing as the thorns hadn't quickly eliminated their target, they were beginning to signal and take formation. They were assembling to create a murder ball.

A murder ball was not only dangerous to a Queen as it is designed to be, but also could harm others close to its center. A large bunch of bees would trap a Queen within their clutches until she became so overheated, she died. Sometimes other bees died within these balls as well. It was a possible suicide mission. It was used when a group of bees decided that the Queen was no longer serving them, and she must be replaced with a new Queen.

They encompassed the hive leaders with alarming speed, and Royal wasn't able to avert them. Amidst the chaos of buzzing, a clear voice projected. "You have not been stewarding this hive as a Queen should. I will do so much better." Without pause, they closed in even more.

Somehow, after buzzing quietly with Sting, Courage was able to slip away before the murder ball formed. He concealed himself into an empty brood cell beside them with amazing speed, and it seemed as if none of their attackers had even taken account of him. Royal turned to Sting with a questioning look, but her King's face didn't betray any thought. It was clear that the three remaining, Royal, Sting, and Nectar, had no more opportunities to escape. So, they inched out of their corner in an attempt to put space between them and Courage's hiding place.

"So, you've taken it upon yourselves to decide what is best for this hive." Royal buzzed, suppressing a wave of fear. Her muffled projection yielded no answer, as the huge crowd of bees were almost upon her. Their faces were oddly unemotional as they finally closed in, and for once, Royal was grateful that she was cold.

The chaos of the murder ball was terrifying, and had the victims been any weaker of mind, they would have been too disoriented to respond. But the three all stood, back to back, solid as a

rock. Royal took a final cool breath as she prepared to use the stinger she possessed. A stinger she rarely used. She thought her deadly weapon might prolong their chances of survival. *Survival... no. This is it for me. This is it for Hive Honey Quest. All we've worked for is crashing down.* But still, somewhere within, she held on to hope. She was ready to defend herself and her two closest kindred spirits rather than submit to a quicker, more painless death.

The heat was setting in fast, and the three flinched under the relentless, pelting feet of their hivemates. Royal tried and occasionally succeeded in stinging one, but it didn't make much of a difference. The attackers were chanting all kinds of strange words in chaotic rhythms. "Thelytoky. Thelytoky. Out with the old, in with the new. We are free. We are free. Remove the toxicity. Thelytoky. Thelytoky." Their voices were monotone and cold, as if removed from themselves.

Royal's heartbeat began to grow faster as her temperature was rising. *Please, Lighthive! Don't let this be the end of all hope for my home!* She relaxed her body, trying to slow the rising temperature. She could feel Sting and Nectar failing behind her. The pressure upon them was overwhelming.

As she was on the verge of passing out, Royal felt a gust of cool air. It enlivened her, and the adrenaline in her body gave her a spurt of energy. With fervent dedication, she began kicking, kicking, kicking her way toward that sliver of light. It became easier each moment, and she felt the weight of the ball dwindling. She didn't have the ability to ensure her King and her nurse bee's survival, so she chose to trust that they would be okay. *I must fight for this hive. I can't give up.* With a triumphant shove, she broke away from the ball.

She collapsed on the ground, disoriented by her near death experience. Blinking, she stared in confusion as she saw a small battle going on around her. Hive defense had responded just in time and had actively weakened the murder ball. Even as the help pulled bees from the ball, the NB members turned on them and attacked in response. Their movements were well-practiced and mechanical. NB had been training for this.

Royal spun her head around, searching frantically for Sting and Nectar. To her relief, both of them broke out just after she did, still alive. Hive Honey Quest troops had surrounded them all to protect them from NB. The interjection had successfully caused the cult's plan to fail. *We can do this.* Royal's energy was renewed, knowing that she had also arranged preparations for a battle such as this. Courage had clearly been successful in calling all hive troops to service. He saved their lives.

Royal had never been in the midst of battle before. It was not a Queen's job. But, she stood fiercely with Nectar right at her side, prepared to defend herself. She glanced admiringly at her King, as he fought with valor and skill. No one could match his prowess.

There were more troops in the hive than there were in NB. As the minutes dragged on, the hive had more and more control of the battle, and the attackers could not withstand their strength. Slowly, every NB member on this mission was restrained by a large, strong drone, and workers thickened the battlefield, prepared to seize any stragglers who might try to escape. Toward the front of the prisoners, a furious worker who wore a monarch butterfly wing as a cape struggled loudly. "No! NOOOOOO!" She screamed without end. "NOOO!"

Royal and Sting strode toward the bee. *This must be Sun.* The Monarch continued to resist to no avail against her captor's strength, spitting on the ground. Royal drew herself to her full height before Sun. "I hereby decree the banishment of Sun and all leaders of NB excluding the informant, Hope. They will be removed from the hive after they reveal the whereabouts of three informants, Hope, Pea, and Thistle. Neither NB leader shall be welcome to return at any point in the future, should they survive."

Sun looked at the Queen with fiery eyes. "You can't undo what has been done. I have changed the hearts of many who dwell in this hive. They will not simply forget their desires and values."

Sting, who stood at the Queen's side, buzzed sternly. "We don't expect or require that everybee agrees with our beliefs. Of course we hope that our hive mates will find freedom and truth, but it must be of their own accord. Each being has their own free will to decide their path, so long as it doesn't destroy the livelihood of the hive, as you have tried to do."

A few of the NB workers and drones managed to escape their foes just then and tried to retreat to a corner of the hive, but they were promptly intercepted into stronger arms. The battle scene had given way to stillness, as they awaited Royal's command on how to proceed. "Each NB member who moved to attack us today should be temporarily held behind bars until we can sort out this mess." The crowd began moving slowly away from the Queen in response to her orders. To a few available workers, she added, "We must extract the other leaders promptly. Bring them and Sun into my interrogation room. Then, we must locate the private honey stores. They may be our only hope for survival. Keep an eye out for Hope, Pea, and Thistle as well while you do. I hope we can get information from the leaders to help us find our lost friends. It may be our only real chance." She added, "Anyone else, please begin clearing away the dead." She gazed sullenly at the bodies scattered on the ground.

Royal sighed soberly, turning to Nectar. Courage had also joined them, and the Queen managed to muster a smile of relief and gratitude. "Courage and Nectar, I'm afraid your mentorship will be more needed than ever to help rehabilitate these cult members. We must appoint others to help in the process." Taking a moment to recover from the ambush and her adrenaline, Royal sighed. At last, their hidden foe had surfaced. Royal had never felt the green light to act, and instead, she had to wait until they acted towards her. Lighthive watched over the battle and kept them safe. It felt as though the pressure of waiting and worrying was finally over, and the hive would only become safer now. After allowing herself a brief moment to breath, she stood tall with resolve. *I am going to help Sting get the information necessary to find Hope.*

Chapter 20: Propolis

Several bees were tied and seated in nutshell chairs in the center of the room. Sting and a few other strapping drones circled them menacingly, as Royal sat near the back to listen. Among the bees seated was Sun, four old leading workers, an old leading drone, and the younger worker and drone recruited with Hope. The lot maintained mostly unphased expressions despite their obvious defeat.

Sting spoke sternly. "All of you are destined to perish in the frost tonight. Before you do, you have the chance to clear your conscience. Where are the informants?" He eyed them each one by one. "Hope, Pea, and Thistle. What have you done with them?"

An older worker hissed, "Just as you deal with us, we have dealt with our traitors."

"You seem to enjoy making your comparisons, as if you believe you've done nothing wrong. And yet, you've done the very thing that goes against design. You've aimed to kill your own Queen, even while she is still functioning and effective." Sting buzzed protectively. "You should have been the victim of her sting."

Walking down the line, he reached the younger drone. Normally tough as nails, the drone was sweating and breaking character. Sting stared him down. Sensing within the drone a softness somewhere deep down, he allowed a trace of pleading desperation to dwell in his gaze. At that, the drone broke. "They are all nearby..." he stammered, trembling.

The other members erupted into loud buzzing. "Zip it!" "Shut it, newbie!" "Don't dishonor me!"

Sting silenced them with a threatening stomp. "Silence! I'd like to hear more, young sir."

The drone twisted uncomfortably in his chair, burning under the glares of his comrades. He wouldn't speak again. Silently, Sting and one of his helpers carried the young drone's chair into a separate attached room. They closed the door, and proceeded their questioning alone. It seemed like they were getting important information out of him.

Royal stared at the leaders of NB. She didn't know exactly what to feel. These bees were able to twist and manipulate one's own thinking to gain the upper hand. They could garner hoards of followers willing to kill for their cause. And they had done it all so gradually. She remembered when Pollen had shared knowledge about NB. Sweet Pea had raised concerns about the group, and had accounted for Hope's attendance. Pollen had then decided to investigate further. At the time, she had concluded that while the group felt off, she didn't believe it to be an active threat. She felt they had no grounds to stop the meetings or otherwise interfere.

In such a short amount of time, just a few months, it had progressed to this. Royal reflected gravely on the day that Hope came to her. For the last many weeks, she repeatedly risked her own life to protect her family. Each day, she took the chance at being discovered, and each day, the group became more radical and dangerous. Now, she may be lost forever.

The silence in the room was loud. Interrupting Royal's thoughts, Sun buzzed quietly. "What an odd girl. I never thought Hope would have it in her to put others above herself. And now, she's in a lot of pain for it."

Royal stood rigid, resisting the urge to speak.

Having not roused the Queen, Sun continued. "Her friends… how patient with her they have been. If I were them, she would have been gone long ago." The Monarch let out a giddy laugh. "She is a lot like me in ways, innately destined to elevate herself. But unlike me, she was not worthy of it."

Royal spoke so quietly, she almost whispered. "She is nothing like you. When faced with her own failures, she chose to do the right thing. She chose to sacrifice her pride, comfort, and safety to protect her friends. To protect what is right. In the end, she will always be remembered for that bravery."

"You give the girl too much credit, Queen. She was fickle."

"She submitted to the Light's imposition on her darkness." *In the moments that mattered most.*

At that moment, Sting opened the door. "We have what we need. We can proceed with the exile. However, I do recommend mercy on this drone. He has been very cooperative and has shown signs of true remorse."

Royal paused before nodding. "I trust your judgment, my love. I expect it is already night. We can banish these seven immediately."

The proceedings were strangely ceremonial. Each NB leader to be exiled walked without faltering, completely dedicated to their truth. They knew their chances no longer existed, and had submitted to their punishment without a fight. They carried themselves with pride, like martyrs who saw no justice. The walk to the chute was quiet and unsettling.

One by one, they filed out of the single-bee tunnel designed for removing the dead from the hive during Flowersleep. Each passed through the tunnel without resistance. Sun was last, and she fixed her eye on her handler with enough coldness to unnerve anybee. In her eye, a determination dwelled that could perhaps defeat even that imminent frost. It sent a chill down her captor's back before she slipped away into the darkness.

Meanwhile, Sting and his troops had invaded the New Beginning quarters. There, hundreds of bees lay in wait, keeping themselves warm. Most were fearful and submissive as the outsiders searched for the missing honey and the informants. While the members didn't interfere, they also did little to help. It was almost as if their heads were in a fog.

Their whole world was shattering in front of them, and they appeared completely baseless and terrified. Some of the members resigned to throwing themselves out the same way their leaders went, into the unforgiving frost. Others huddled quietly, shivering, and staring blankly into the shadows.

After the attackers had been contained, many search parties went out to find the informants. Even the drone who had been spared of the exile helped however he could, despite his somewhat limited knowledge. Even with every effort, it took days before they came close to finding Hope, Pea, and Thistle.

The private honey stores were found residing in a storage space behind the NB meeting area. Further behind that, a ladder was found that led downward. This ladder led to uncharted space below the hive. It was very cold and dangerous to enter, but in small groups, they were able to search the area little by little. There were halls and tunnels made by bees that led to nowhere. In frustration, the groups searched and searched to no avail. There was not a destination to be found. After some deliberation, they began to destroy the halls to look for sealed off rooms. It was very challenging work. It took many special tools and lots of elbow grease to penetrate this particularly hard solution, which had been determined to be propolis. Such was often used to repair holes in the hive, and it wasn't meant to be easily destroyed. In the cold, it had become so brittle that it was a gnarly opponent.

It had been three or four days since the attack before they found what they had been searching for. With a sudden release, one of the walls shattered, revealing a seamless prison. Sweet Pea and Thistle were curled up on the floor. Nearby, a bee shouted that they had simultaneously discovered Hope's cell. With great haste, the three bodies were carried up the ladder to the warmth of the throne room with Royal.

Nectar watched the bodies closely while some workers generated heat in her operating room. They tried anything they could, hoping it wasn't too late. They didn't know if the prisoners had access to any food for those four days. Royal waited on her throne, her heart racing with anger and anticipation. Sting was at her side. After a few minutes passed, Nectar emerged. She shook her head solemnly, indicating that the three informants had in fact passed away. Royal was crushed, tears pouring as she turned to Sting. She buried her face in his fur, unable to bear the pain of her broken heart.

Chapter 21: A Glimmer of Light

Courage was busy at work, as always. He, Nectar, and a couple others had worked tirelessly to help the NB members recover over the last few weeks. Their minds had been taken advantage of, and they desperately needed to fill the void somehow. He had learned so much about the cult members just by listening to them talk. They sought something real, and they thought they had found just that. Many spoke only well of the group and its direction. It would likely be months before they would think for themselves again, and if they didn't have support, they would quickly be attracted to other similar groups to find a sense of community and purpose. Courage gently and carefully reminded them of who they were without NB. Eventually, many would truly heal and recover from the experience.

Several bees in the hive were assigned the creative task of building a memorial for Hope, Pea, and Thistle - one of them being Joy. The trios' funeral had been simple and brief due to the difficult times, and Royal had decided that their bravery should never be forgotten. In the whirlwind of events, no one had been allowed a moment to really grieve the losses. This was one way their memory could be preserved and honored. It was in fact very possibly thanks to their sacrifice that Royal was still alive and reigning.

In a small lull between events, Courage approached the creative group as they worked on their design in the landing grounds. Just one look at her brother, and Joy leapt in excitement. "Brother! Oh how I've missed you!"

The two took a moment's rest together. Words failed them as they stood silent and solemn. After a long pause, Joy spoke.

"This hive is hurting, Courage. I can feel it."

Courage nodded. "Yes. It is."

"It really surprised me to hear about how New Beginning became so dangerous. I knew early on that something was off, but I couldn't have even imagined how they'd threaten our very livelihood. How did they convince others to follow them?"

Courage paused, then buzzed in response. "After oppression such as Buzzz's era here, it's not surprising. His absence was such a change. Many bees subconsciously wanted structure and rule to replace him. His leaving created a vacuum for something like this to occur."

"But I don't understand. They were free! Why would so many bees, good bees, become subject to something so bad?"

"Not every bee has your spidey senses, Joy!" Courage chuckled, before returning to seriousness. "Everybee is susceptible to manipulation, no matter how self-established. New Beginning offered appreciation, acknowledgment, family, support, and purpose. Such are key requirements for a life to flourish. Once they drew in these members and called them their own, it was sealed. The members trusted and believed. Some maybe even feared. They believed that Sun was right and good, and that their happiness and continued membership depended on their compliance. They would do anything - because they believed, and because their own happiness was the highest priority to them. They were deafened to their own gut and conscience."

Joy contemplated. "Doesn't this mean that they'll be seeking a replacement yet again?"

"We are always seeking purpose and true joy. Yes, they will look. And I can only hope that they will find the true source of those things. But in the meantime, we hope to help them reset and rewire their thought process so they can truly heal, and truly be free for the first time. It's going to be quite a journey, but it will be worth it."

"Finally then, peace will envelop this entire hive!" Joy spun around, giddy. "*True* peace, for all. It will be our golden era!"

Courage smiled at his dear sister. "Yes, yes it will. At last, peace will be restored within." The siblings ceased their conversation as the hustle and bustle quieted around them. A small crowd had formed in the landing grounds as they noticed their Queen.

Royal strode to her podium, Sting and Nectar at her side. The three were still tattered from their recent battle, but they were standing strong. Courage, Joy, and everybee in the clearing turned their attention toward her. "Hello all. As you know, New Beginning has ended, and ever since, we've been piecing together our hive from the inside. Thanks to the private honey reserves, we have made it thus far. Normally, Flowersleep drags on for a couple more weeks. However, it did come early this year, and I feel a strange warmth closing in on us this morning." She paused. "Lighthive has shared with Nectar that today, it will be warm enough to forage for spring flowers!"

The crowd was dead silent for a breath before erupting into cheers of celebration. It was a long while before they quieted again.

Royal continued speaking. "You may fly as the sun reaches its peak, and return before it cools. For today, we shall clear part of the entrance away. We should repair it at night before the evening frost returns. Go soak up the sun, and be heartened. All of today's ongoing duties are postponed until tomorrow."

The grounds were abuzz as Royal concluded her speech. A new light shone in each bee's eyes - a light of hope and relief. Joy looked at Courage with happiness. "Shall we?"

The two raced to the hive entrance to help de-patch. The material was softer, as a warmer sun beat down on it. Courage worked away. Thoughts of his long lost teacher, Thistle, filled his mind. Thistle had been such a good friend and mentor, and losing him had been devastating. Every outdoor endeavor with his mentors had been full of adventure and boyish play. Those were core memories. *At least I know I'll be reunited with Thistle again. One day... back where I truly belong.*

Joy piped up as they worked. "Hey, I'm sure you've really missed your special lady friend! Will you try to find her?" Her eyes twinkled with amusement.

"I just might." Courage tried not to blush. "She is too far away for my taste." The two had a laugh. Just then, the clearing had finished, and the hive entrance was considerably opened. Courage and Joy looked at one another before taking off into the blinding light.

The sun was warm, welcoming, and beautiful, and they felt free and peaceful like never before.

THE END

Also by Amarah Parks

Hive Honey Quest
Hope
Faith

Watch for more at https://www.instagram.com/amarahparks/.

About the Author

Amarah enjoys a quiet life in Minnesota with her amazing husband and adorable one year old son. In addition to writing, she enjoys creating and releasing music as well as raising competetive show rabbits.

Read more at https://www.instagram.com/amarahparks/.